Rebel Heart

Night Life – Book One

Dani Petrone

Print ISBNs
Amazon Print 9780228624295
LSI Print 9780228624301
B&N Print 9780228624318

Dedication

My thanks to The Butterscotch Martini Girls for their support, love, and giving me the confidence to sit my butt in a chair and write a book.

Chapter One

My life is a lie. Rebecca Prentice took a deep breath and willed herself to relax. I can do this, she thought. She could smile and pretend everything was fine. It wasn't, and no amount of acting could change the fact her beloved father had an affair with a young co-worker. How could he have done that to her mother, or her for that matter? He'd always emphasized how family values were so important to him. Yeah, right.

Tension throbbed in Rebecca's head. She took a sip of her butterscotch martini and ran her hand underneath the long, blonde wig she wore to massage the back of her neck. As she did, she fixed her gaze on two of her three friends, Rayna and Scarlett. Her third friend, Trisha, was predictably late.

Rebecca and her friends were at the Ritz, a bar and grill near central Phoenix, where they met most Thursdays for happy hour. The Ritz was the local hangout for white-collar professionals. Rebecca often ran into attorneys from her office building or people she'd consulted with on cases at the firm where she was employed as an assistant attorney. Occasionally, she'd met her father, the prominent Senator Prentice, for lunch at the Ritz. Of course, those had been happier days before she'd overheard her parent's whispered conversations. Then his indiscretions went public.

"Are you excited, Rebecca?" Rayna tapped a neon-painted fingernail on the tabletop.

Jostled from her musings, Rebecca blinked and flashed a weak smile. "Sorry. What?"

"Are you excited?" her friend repeated. "About going to a biker bar tonight. We'll have fun. Maybe we'll make a difference in a guy or two's life."

Rebecca winced. She planned to make things different, which was the purpose of the blonde wig and the sexy clothes she wore, just not for a guy. Her statement made perfect sense, but she couldn't voice it out loud. Instead, she muttered, "Yeah, I'm ready."

Taking a deep breath, Rebecca forced aside her personal issues. It wasn't easy, but she'd do it. Growing up in a family where every gesture had to be politically correct, she'd had plenty of practice. What rocked her to her core was finding out her perfect family was a lie.

Sweet, intelligent, and dependable were words used to describe Rebecca. No one had ever imagined her as a 'wild' woman. In her twenty-six years of life, never once had she thought of getting herself into trouble. Even in college, when a guy asked her out, or friends invited her to a party, she'd often turned them down. Her entire focus had been to study hard and ensure her grades pleased her parents. Well, what had that got her? A life that now seemed empty…or, a better word, boring.

She'd only shown backbone when she rejected the expected 'join the Junior League' much to her parent's protest and volunteered at Haven of Peace, a local women's shelter. It pleased her that she was helping make lives better for others in abused situations or who were temporarily down on their luck.

Rebecca ran a finger along the stem of her martini glass while deep in thought. I can become someone different, she told herself. Of course, she realized she couldn't change the past, but she could change her future. Become a new Rebecca. She had no idea who this new Rebecca could be, but in her heart, she knew it was time to shed the cocoon of her designer suits and heirloom pearls.

"Come on, Rebecca." Her friend, Rayna, had pleaded.

"It will be fun. You'll meet your Mr. Right." Scarlett had told her.

Trisha had added to the conversation. "It's a great plan, Rebecca."

The plan was to check out various bars dressed in different personalities to find their Mr. Right. Rebecca immediately had rejected the idea. Pretending to be someone else wouldn't help her situation. Besides, she wasn't ready to look for a Mr. Right, not yet anyway. First, she had to discover her new personality. Plus, as a senator's daughter, and a newly hired assistant attorney, the last thing she needed was to get herself in a situation and end up a headline in the morning news. Their family already had enough bad publicity, thanks to her father.

After mulling the idea over, Rebecca decided a disguise could give her a chance to go out and not be recognized. Wearing different clothing than her usual style and putting on various colors of wigs, she'd walk into the world and enjoy the possibilities. After all, it had to be better than sitting around feeling sorry for herself.

So far, she hadn't found her new persona, but at least she'd stepped from her comfort zone. And she hadn't been recognized.

For the first time in her life, Rebecca felt freedom.

Rebecca's thoughts drifted back to the first night they'd put their plan into action. She smiled remembering how they'd checked out a goth bar called Free Harmony. The place was packed with ghoulish-dressed people partying like vampires to the loud music. She'd enjoyed a delicious concoction of chartreuse and gin from a tall silver goblet and danced until her feet were numb. But Rebecca left the night club knowing she wouldn't be coming back. As much fun as she'd had, the goth bar was only a one-time adventure.

A few weeks later, she and her friends dressed in denim and rhinestones and headed to Cave Creek in search of a cowboy bar. It hadn't taken long to find one. Lazy Jake's western-themed bar had plenty of good-looking men and great country music. Rebecca learned to line dance, and the instructor told her she showed a natural talent. Oh, she'd been flattered, but still, she hadn't felt entirely comfortable.

Tonight, their plan was to find a bar frequented by bikers. Which reminded her, could she get a butterscotch martini in a biker bar?

"By the way, Rebecca, you look sensational," Scarlett stated. "You may find a special man tonight. Someone who'll ease the pain your family is causing and bring some fun into your life." Her words seemed tinged with a touch of mischief.

Oh, boy, she was doomed if it was going to take a man to make her life better. These girls had no idea how hard the past few weeks had been. Still, it wasn't as though she didn't want a man in her life. She did. But

Rebecca also knew she couldn't trust herself. She was much too naive regarding personal relationships, which made absolutely no sense because reading body language at the office was one of her strong points. She knew immediately when a client wasn't being truthful.

Rebecca speculated it must be a family trait to miss the signs in your own life. After all, her mother hadn't realized her father was a liar and a cheater. She bit her lower lip.

As memories surfaced, the familiar lump of emotion began to form in her throat. The tightness happened every time she thought of her father and his indiscretions. If only pretending could change the past. It couldn't. She knew that, but she would deal with it differently than her mother. Her fingers circled the stem of her martini glass. She was tired of being a milquetoast to keep up appearances. She could speak her truth. She could become someone new. After all, she was a rebel at heart. Wasn't she?

Rebecca cleared her throat and shrugged. "I seriously doubt dressing up in different outfits will make me forgive my father, but, who knows, maybe I'll discover something new about myself in a biker bar. Find out who I am without being told what to wear and how to act. I'll be a new Reb—"

"That's our girl!" Rayna interrupted, "Did you notice our waiter drooling when he dropped off our drinks?"

Rebecca laughed. "I bet he doesn't see many outfits like this in here." She leaned forward to give her friends a better view of her cleavage. "It's definitely not Ritz attire." The black leather halter with sheer lace inserted across the deep V-neck didn't leave much to the imagination. The salesclerk at the boutique said it was perfect to wear to a biker bar.

The top certainly wasn't modest, but Rebecca liked how it made her feel. Sexy, alluring, and most of all, different. Exactly what she wanted...different. She'd bought it without giving additional thought to the purchase. Plus, a pair of low-riding jeans, low enough to show the recently acquired butterfly tattoo her friends had dared her to get.

Rebecca never backed down from a dare, especially after a couple of tequila shots. Getting the tattoo hurt like the devil, but she'd suffered through the process. It had been her step number one on the way to becoming a new Rebecca. She shifted slightly in her seat and lifted her martini glass in a salutation.

"To us!" Rebecca said.

"To us!" Scarlett and Rayna repeated in unison.

As the girls chatted among themselves, Rebecca turned her attention toward the girl sitting next to her with pink-streaked hair. Rayna was one of her college roommates and a good friend for over five years. Rayna had dressed for the night in skinny jeans, knee-high black boots, and a white T-shirt with a skull and angel wings printed on the back. She looked stunning.

Maybe, just maybe, if I can show even half the flair this wild adventurer demonstrates, I'll be on my way toward becoming the new 'wild' Rebecca, she thought while letting out a deep sigh.

Rayna obviously overheard the exhale and leaned in close to Rebecca's ear. "You look...perky."

Perky? Cool! Rebecca congratulated herself. "Thanks. I can go with perky." At least she knew how to select the right wardrobe. Maybe she was meant to be a biker chick. Wouldn't that be a hoot? She'd certainly give her family a shock if it were true.

I wonder, she thought. What would it be like to ride on a motorcycle? Have the wind blow across my face, hold tight to a rugged good-looking man with a definite wild side.

"Rebecca, in that outfit, you'll have every guy in the place drooling." Scarlett's voice cracked with laughter. The movement of her head sent a spray of multi-colored glitter raining around her newly permed hair. Scarlett never left the house without tossing a generous handful of glitter over her body, and tonight it looked like she'd thrown an extra handful into her reddish-brown curls.

"What about you, Scarlett?" Rebecca changed the subject. "Who would have ever expected you to find a man in a cowboy bar?"

"Right," Rayna echoed. "I didn't see that one coming." She laughed. "Scarlett finds her man in the cowboy bar. Next, she'll wear a pair of spurs decorated with fairy wings."

"Hey, not a bad idea," Scarlett added with a lift of her eyebrows.

"Oh, yeah, I can see it all now," Rayna said.

Rebecca couldn't help but laugh and shake her head. How could anyone stay unhappy while keeping company with these women? Recovering her composure, she had to ask again, "You're sure this outfit isn't too revealing? I don't want to look slutty." She cupped her breasts, covering her cleavage with her spread fingers.

"Sorry I'm late, girls." Trisha, the last to arrive as predicted, her long dark hair flowing wildly over her shoulders, scooted into the empty chair. "What have I missed?"

"Not much. Rebecca's concerned about her boobs," Scarlett offered, her expression clearly showing amusement.

Trisha signaled to the cute blond waiter to bring her the usual, then turned her attention toward Rebecca. "What's wrong with your tits?"

"Oh, my god, nothing's wrong with them." Rebecca sat up straighter. She felt her cheeks heat as she swept her hand across her chest. "I'm worried I'm showing too much cleavage, that's all. Geesh, you girls." She shook her head.

She hoped that sounded convincing. If her friends had any idea how badly she was floundering on her quest to change her persona, they'd certainly be compassionate. But she couldn't keep expecting them to bolster her spirits while she tried to figure out who she truly was. This was something she had to do on her own.

Their server returned to the table and placed a margarita in front of Trisha. As he did, his eyes roamed across Rebecca's cleavage again. Rebecca's throat tightened, uncomfortable from the attention. "I'll have another." She slid her fingers to the edge of her glass and glanced around the table. The others smiled and confirmed they were also ready for a second round. Plus, a plate of appetizers.

Their server nodded and turned toward the bar to put in their order.

Trisha waited until he was out of earshot before picking up the conversation about Rebecca's attire. "You know, Rebecca, you need a man more than a new personality. Relax a little and enjoy the attention."

"Yeah, if you're looking for a man, you want your boobies to show." Scarlett teased. She lifted her glass and swallowed. The movement caused her silver, dangling fairy earrings to tinkle.

"And she should know. Miss, I think I'll ride me a cowboy." Rayna winked at Scarlett and then quickly returned her attention to the others.

"I'll ignore that remark." Scarlett's cheeks matched the pink streaks in Rayna's hair.

"What about the guy with the black spiked hair, Trisha?" Rayna asked as she checked her cell phone for messages and then dropped it back into her purse. "Lord, girl, what were you thinking?"

Trisha glanced up and shrugged. "I was thinking I loved him."

"Should we ask?" Rayna's brown eyes twinkled.

"Nope." A smile teased Trisha's rose, glossed lips. Then a low chuckle escaped her throat. "Remind me sometime to tell you what a tongue ring can do."

"Oh, my goodness." Rebecca breathed.

"You girls don't know what you're missing." Trisha countered confidently.

They all broke into uncontrollable laughter.

There, right there. That's the difference between my friends and myself, Rebecca thought. Trisha had no issue talking about her night with the tongue-ring guy, and the other two didn't seem to have any problems deciding when their next man would show up.

The waiter returned with their drink orders, fussed with the appetizer plate, refilled water glasses then moved away from the table.

"So, everyone is really okay with this outfit?" Rebecca hooked her thumbs under the straps of her tight leather top to pull it up higher. Letting go of the straps, she reached for her second butterscotch martini, enjoying the sparkle of the familiar diamond bracelet she'd worn since graduating from private school.

"You look like Paris Hilton in that long platinum wig. No one will suspect you're the daughter of the infamous Senator Prentice." Rayna took a coconut shrimp off the appetizer plate and bit off a healthy bite.

Rebecca frowned. "I hope not. And thanks for liking this look," she said while finger combing through the long, silky strands. Maybe the platinum wig was the right idea for tonight. She looked like a different person. She took a deep breath and straightened in her chair. Yes, I will change. I will become someone new.

"I liked the cowgirl Becky Jo persona." Trisha turned toward Scarlett. "Didn't you?"

Scarlett shrugged. "Rebecca looked fabulous with red hair."

"That didn't work out so well," Rebecca reminded them. At the cowboy bar, Rebecca had dressed in denim and rhinestones and called herself Becky Jo. However, even though she'd had a great time, she'd felt a bit out of place. "That wasn't the real me, after all. When we get to the biker bar, you'll see a new Rebecca."

"As opposed to the other 'new' Rebecca," Rayna asked, "who wore a straight black wig and called herself Becca at the Free Harmony Goth bar?"

Rebecca had to laugh. Scarlett had suggested the popular Goth bar hoping to find her perfect match, only low and behold, Trisha, the cowgirl—who never looked twice at any man without a Stetson—was the one who found her man.

At the Free Harmony bar, Rebecca had tried to fit in with her friends. The gold tank top with sparkles and a black wig had looked fantastic, but still, it hadn't seemed natural.

"That didn't work out so well either," Rebecca admitted. "At least at the cowboy bar I found...oh, never mind."

Trisha looked over toward her friend. "I detect someone has details to share?" A smile tugged at her gorgeous lips.

"I won't bore you with the specifics," she muttered.

The nice-looking cowboy had offered to buy her breakfast, then talked nonstop about himself and how many bulls he'd ridden. Suspecting the only bull he'd experienced was the bull he fed her, Rebecca had slipped out as quickly as she could and hustled home. Finally, comfortable in her silk pajamas and snuggled between her Ralph Lauren designer sheets, she'd fallen asleep the moment her head hit the pillow.

"Too small, huh?" Scarlett chuckled.

"Geesh, Scarlett. No." She fought a burst of laughter. "Oh, I don't know, he was...." Not right, but how did she explain her feelings when she didn't understand them herself? All she knew was that she'd been amazed at their colorful personalities since her first day with this group of women. "For lack of a better word, he was boring." *Just like me*, she thought.

"All right, enough of this," Rayna interrupted. "Rebecca, you look hot, and you know it. Actually, we all look hot." She stood, slipped her denim jacket off the chair, and picked up her handbag. "Ladies, I have a surprise." She practically bounced up and down as she boasted proudly, "My cousin owns a cool bar—it's called Mo's—he's offered us drinks on the house." Her smile widened. "We'll have a good time because his bar rocks. And it's a common place for bikers to hang out."

Rebecca swirled her finger around the rim of her martini glass to scoop up the last taste of butterscotch. "Sounds fantastic. Remember, my name is Reb."

Maybe tonight, she told herself, would prove, as Reb, she was a wild adventurer.

She already knew she wasn't as breezy as Scarlett, as insouciant as Trisha, or as devil-may-care as Rayna. Even so, she suspected the odds of meeting a Mr. Right at a biker bar weren't too good. The bar at the Ritz, full of men with the kind of money she was used to, was still the only place she felt completely at home.

"Tonight will be different," Rebecca vowed as they left the Ritz. "I'm going to be crazy, daring, and adventurous. I will release my wild side when I enter the biker bar as Reb. Besides, no one will recognize me in this get-up, so what could go wrong?"

Chapter Two

Tonight, Mo's bar was busier than usual. Mick Harris almost didn't notice the group of women at the corner table until Danny pointed them out. But as soon as the drummer nodded in their direction with the 'get a look' expression Mick recognized as 'hot chicks in the house,' he found it hard to concentrate on the words he sang.

They'd played the number half a dozen times this year. Every night Mick filled in for the lead guitarist, keyboard guy, or even the sax man, so it shouldn't be hard to keep his mind on the music. But something about the group in the corner kept drawing his gaze back to them, and when it did, he'd miss a word.

Maybe it was the glitter-dusted brunette whose laugh carried across the room. The lady with the long dark hair was giving off a 'not interested' vibe, which narrowed down the choices somewhat, but then there was the blonde in the corner. She looked as if she'd rather be anyplace else in the world.

Interesting group, Mick thought as they segued into Fever Road. The chick with the pink-streaked hair had possibly been here last time he'd stood in for Earl or Jax because she looked familiar. And while none of her friends seemed the type he usually saw at Mo's, they appeared to be enjoying the show just fine.

All except for the blonde.

"Harris?"

The bar manager beckoned him from the side of the platform that served as a stage. At least the guy had waited until Danny's drum solo. Every so often, somebody would request a song from the manager instead of standing up and shouting "Joyride" or "Natchez Down" or whatever they wanted to hear.

It annoyed him to get requests from the boss because the whole point of playing music in a biker bar was escaping the formality of his nine-to-five life. For a few crazy hours, three or four nights a month, he could put aside his computer and Armani suits, his case files, and Michael W. Harris business cards to get lost in the world of music. Sending messages through managers was the kind of thing tax attorneys expected at Marks, Taylor & Cohn…hell, he did it himself. At Mo's, he wished people would yell their requests from the floor. Wild and crazy, that's what Mick wanted.

Still, it was the lead vocalist's job to take requests. Since that was Mick tonight, he moved toward the manager while Danny pounded away on the drums.

"Yeah?" He shouted over the beat of the drums.

"Table in the corner wants a song for the blonde."

Interesting. Such requests were usually for someone celebrating a birthday, a divorce, or some other milestone, but the blonde didn't look like she'd come to Mo's to celebrate. Oh, she was trying to fit in—she had the same number of shot glasses and beer mugs as everyone else. He saw her smiling at one of her friends, but even from this far away, he could tell her smile was an effort.

Probably a divorce, then. Mick hoped he could remember the song Jax had offered last time they got such a request because no matter how well Rafe and Earl knew the music, they couldn't fill in on vocals.

"Okay. Got it covered." Yeah, he knew exactly what to sing to a beautiful lady. Soon as Danny's solo wound down, he'd signal to the guys. No point waiting, especially when it'd give him a closer look at the corner table.

Mick realized the women must have been expecting him as soon as he started toward them. All, except for the blonde, began nudging each other. As he drew closer and got his first glimpse of the lace-and-leather barely covering her nipples, he found himself wondering if he'd been wrong about her not fitting in.

His gaze went a little higher to stare straight into a pretty face surrounded by waves of long blonde hair. A face any musician could fantasize about while writing a song. His breath hitched. She sure looked like she belonged here.

Now, if he could get her to smile for him...

"Look who's heading our way," Rayna announced.

Rebecca sat up a little straighter. Had her friend already spotted the perfect man?

The one headed in their direction sure looked perfect. This man wasn't as shaggy-haired as the other guys in the band, even though his clothes were the same casual combination as everyone else's. But the way his jeans fit and the faded T-shirt under his leather vest rested against his skin showed her biker bar musicians weren't quite as seedy as she'd expected.

In fact, if you put this dark-haired man in a three-piece suit tailored for his broad shoulders, he'd probably look right at home in the Ritz.

Stop it! Rebecca ordered herself. She was Reb tonight, and Reb didn't miss the Ritz or butterscotch martinis one bit. Reb was perfectly happy drinking beer and throwing back shots at Mo's, just like her friends.

Rebecca watched the singer approach their table with such keen anticipation she felt her skin tighten. It was almost as if something incredible was about to happen. But what could happen in a place like Mo's? It wasn't her kind of bar. Unless maybe she'd finally discovered the right persona. As he stepped closer to their table, she hoped it to be accurate more fiercely. But no, even if Mo's were where the new Rebecca belonged, a guy from a biker bar band would, undoubtedly, have his eyes on Rayna. Not on herself.

He gazed leisurely at them, from Scarlett to Rayna to Trisha, and then he fixed his attention on her.

He held out his hand.

Rebecca's heartbeat quickened. Without a second thought, she stood and put her hand in his.

"You're beautiful," he said softly. His voice was both rough and smooth, just like his shadowed jaw.

There came a swirl of music. A song, right, but he wasn't exactly singing it. He was speaking to her.

"Tonight. Who knew…I'd find you here tonight?" He pulled her in close, and they began to move to the beat. "Waiting for so long, for someone…for you."

He cinched her tighter and executed a perfect turn. She stayed with him as if they floated above the dance floor in a cosmic bubble containing nothing but themselves.

And the music.

And the scent of his skin.

"Waiting…for you. So beautiful." He was singing the words into his microphone while gazing directly at her. Her body began to tingle. She couldn't look away. In his eyes, she felt beautiful, and he was so handsome. His face, his eyes, his body. She could see the heat flickering in his deep, blue eyes, feel the warmth of his skin as he leaned closer and closer.

"Beautiful tonight."

Delicious sizzling sensations raced through her as they continued to sway, just her and this man, lost in a haze of music, feelings, and warmth. Such warmth. She knew her skin was flushed, and she knew his was as well. She felt the heat radiating between them, and for a wild moment, she wondered if they'd spark into flames on the dance floor. Like characters from an animated cartoon, they'd become a mixture of colors and float away forever lost. She let out a soft sigh.

"Who knew…just you…?"

Something about this man held her suspended in time, in space, in everything except for the pulsing warmth she could feel, drawing them closer and closer. Maybe this was what her friends meant by the perfect man, or at least part of it—the raw physical yearning for every aspect of him, right here and now.

Obviously, she couldn't rip her clothes off and throw herself at him, could she? Not while he was singing to her on a dance floor in a crowded bar. All she could do was melt with each word, each glance, and new crest of heat burning between them.

"Because you're beautiful...tonight."

It took her a moment to realize the music had stopped, and she only noticed because her girlfriends, along with the bar crowd, began applauding. Rebecca couldn't move, and apparently, he couldn't either. He stood still, staring at her as if he couldn't turn away.

Then she heard one of the guys from the stage shout, "Hey, Mick, how about Road Ode Mama?" She saw his surprise start, realizing that the lead singer couldn't stand in the middle of the dance floor holding a woman all night. And the agonizing force of will he seemed to need to jerk his gaze from her, escort her to her friends, smile, and head back to the stage.

Rebecca slid into her chair and watched the man she had danced with walk away. He's fantastic, she thought.

"Hmm," said Trisha. "Reb, you might want to keep that wig."

"Wig? Oh, right."

"We should come here more often," purred Rayna. "My cousin will send us a different singer every night."

Her cousin? The owner had sent this singer to their table!

"He'll have a hard time finding someone better than that guy," Trisha murmured. "Check out his tight ass. I'd take him home in a heartbeat."

Acting? The guy had been acting. What a dope I am. Oh, my god.

Rebecca couldn't believe what had happened. She'd fallen for his charm like a naive teenager. She'd actually thought he was attracted to her—the egotistical jerk. He's probably bragging with his band buddies about how the little groupie fell all over him. Rebecca gritted her teeth. Oh, who cares. He wasn't the kind of man she wanted anyway.

But even though no biker-bar band guy would ever be that man, and as much as she'd like to punch him in his arrogant nose, she felt herself blush remembering his touch. That angered her even more.

"We need another round," Scarlett turned to look for a waitress. At that moment, a bottle flew past their table, barely missing her head. "Whoa!" She ducked, grabbing Rebecca by the arm as she went down.

One crash was followed by another, then by too many to count.

"Fight time!" Someone yelped from the other side of the room.

Rayna jumped from her chair and hopped onto the shoulders of a big burly man wearing a Grateful Dead T-shirt and began swinging a long-neck beer bottle over her head like a lariat.

"Rayna, no!" Rebecca pleaded. "Someone, do something. She's going to get hurt."

"Oh, yeah. I'm getting in on this," Trisha shouted. She dived under the nearest pool table after grabbing a cue stick from someone and started whacking at the ankles of the fighting men with it.

Rebecca shrank back into the corner as far as she could, her heart hammering in her chest. Scarlett didn't share her idea of the best place to hide. She hurried from her chair and made a mad dash toward the back door.

Rebecca tried to focus on what was happening around her, but it was hard. She couldn't think straight. None of those proper behavior classes for politicians' children had ever covered a fight in a biker bar

"Come on, Rebecca!"

She heard Scarlett call, but her muscles wouldn't respond. Her body stayed frozen in her seat. Then a bottle shattered against the wall behind her. Shielding her face with her hands, Rebecca pressed herself against the back of her chair, closed her eyes, and screamed as a shower of glass cascaded over her hair and shoulders.

Two men fell across her table, still trading blows.

"I've got you."

Still shielding her face, she opened her eyes enough to see the guy from the band reaching for her. Knocking the fighting bikers out of the way, he swept her into his arms.

Rebecca gripped him tight and buried her face against his shoulder as he carried her straight out the front door.

The parking lot was almost as noisy as the bar, but all she could hear was his voice, the deep baritone that covered her like soft, warm cashmere.

"It's okay. I've got you. You're okay."

As he held her, all the anger she'd felt for him faded. Suddenly everything was more than okay. She wanted to stay in this man's warm embrace all night. Although maybe not in the parking lot. And neither did he. She could tell by how fiercely he held her, how hard he was breathing, and how hungrily he now gazed at her lips.

Leaning close, he whispered, "I'm Mick."

"Reb." She barely chocked out the words.

"Well, Reb, may I give you a ride home?"

Oh, yes. Rebecca blinked. Oh, wait. Her friends. They had a pact never to leave anyone behind. She needed to find them and see if they were okay. Plus make them aware she was letting this man give her a ride home.

She quickly scanned the parking lot and found them standing beside Scarlett's car smiling and waving. She didn't have to say anything. They already suspected she was going to have fun tonight somewhere else besides with them.

She turned her gaze back to the handsome hunk of a man still holding her. That would be nice, thank you, she almost answered before remembering her new persona. Reb probably wouldn't talk that way. But Rebecca had no idea what a cool biker chick would say. Before she could give it more thought, she blurted, "you can do anything you want."

Chapter Three

As the warm night wind whipped through the strands of synthetic blonde hair, Rebecca decided Mick was her knight-in-shining-armor. Although, Knight in black leather was a more accurate description. Right now, she was heading toward her house on his Harley-Davidson motorcycle. Except for the bar fight, this was her fantasy come true.

What a crazy night. First, she'd dressed up in clothes usually not her style. Second, she found herself in the middle of a bar fight. Now she was on a motorcycle allowing a guy from a band she only knew as Mick to take her home. Not to mention less than an hour earlier, she'd never wanted to see him again.

The way her shoulder hurt, she probably had a chunk of glass in it from a broken beer bottle. Lord. If her parents could see her now. They'd be mortified. She smiled and whispered to herself, "Would serve them right."

"You okay, Reb?"

"Oh, I'm doing great."

She tightened her grip around Mick's waist, leaned closer to his muscular back, closed her eyes, and breathed in his scent. Sudden warmth spread through her belly.

"Except my shoulder hurts. I think a broken bottle cut it."

"I'll take a look as soon as we get to your place."

"Turn left at the light."

What was it about this man? She barely knew him. She'd already pegged him as a bad boy, yet her imagination kept wondering what it would be like if he kissed her...or more.

She couldn't deny something electrifying ignited between them earlier. The sparks had burst into flames as Mick sang to her at Mo's. Rebecca didn't do bar hookups. But he was just so dang good-looking. Mick changed lanes causing her to grip him tighter. The feel of his muscular body set off a heated reaction within her again.

Her body was betraying her rational mind. However, you know what? She argued to calm the panic tearing through her. She was supposed to be a new Rebecca. Besides, it had been a long time since she'd had sex. Maybe a one-night stand would be an excellent idea. Oh, yes, it was a fantastic idea. And why not, with a guy like Mick, a bad-boy musician who wasn't looking for a relationship? No strings, no commitment, and nothing to worry about later. Just a big win-win.

I'll have excitement and adventure, and tomorrow he'll be on his way. Back to Mo's and on to his next woman. Rebecca dismissed the flash of sadness that accompanied her thoughts.

Mick slowed the Harley and pulled up to the gated entrance. She had to release her grip to punch in the code. When the gate opened, she grabbed his waist again and leaned against him until she instructed him to turn right at the second driveway.

He eased into her private driveway and stopped long enough for her to slide from her position on the padded seat. She stood on shaky legs while Mick parked the bike.

"Next time I take you for a ride, you're wearing a helmet. I don't care if Arizona law says it's not a requirement."

Next time? She smiled, "We'll see."

Rebecca's gaze ran the length of the biker guy who stood at least six-foot-one. The arousal already coursing through her veins deepened. Oh, yes, I'd like another time.

"Want to come inside?"

His face lit up with her invitation. "Thanks. I should look at that shoulder of yours."

"It does still hurt."

Rebecca didn't stop to think about how her high-priced condo screamed 'pampered princess' instead of 'biker chick' until they got halfway up the walk to her front door. She glanced toward him, and he didn't seem to notice the contrast between her outfit and home. Either that, or he didn't care. Or maybe there wasn't a difference. Her parents thought that bikers only spent their money on motorcycle parts and beer was wrong. Anyone could love to ride a motorcycle. She had certainly enjoyed it. One didn't have only to love luxury cars and diamonds.

At the front door, she realized she didn't have a key. "Oh, no, I left my purse at Mo's. Hopefully, it's still there tomorrow. It's a Coach."

"If Mo found it, you can be sure he'll keep it safe. He's honest as anyone you'll ever meet."

Rebecca shrugged. "Good to know. Still, it could have ended up anywhere in tonight's mess."

"Mo's can get rowdy on occasion."

"Yes, I found that out," she mumbled.

Bending down next to a large green and black concrete frog sitting at the edge of the front patio, she found what she needed. The spare key hid underneath the frog's fat bottom in case of an emergency. Turning toward Mick, she held the key up proudly. "I knew this might come in handy someday. Of course, I never thought it would be from forgetting my purse in a biker bar." She laughed.

A smile tipped the corners of his lips, and Mick moved aside to let her unlock the door.

She stuck the key in the lock and turned the knob. "I haven't been home since early morning. The place is a little messy." Rebecca hesitated for a second, then took a deep breath. Was she going to invite this handsome stranger into her home?

Last chance to chicken out.

She pushed open the door and stepped into the plush foyer.

Mick followed right behind her.

I shouldn't have told him my place is a mess. That's too much like the old Rebecca. Her new personality shouldn't care about making a good impression. Reb is a take me as I am woman. Tough. Strong. In control. What you see is what you get. Heck, maybe Reb liked a messy house. Nope, that's going a bit too far. No one likes a mess.

The click of the door behind them jarred her from her thoughts. The sound also told her Mick had turned the lock. They were alone.

Entirely alone. Her heartbeat sped up.

All Rebecca's internal alarms started to ring. After all, he was almost a stranger. What if he was an ax murderer? Nope, been watching too many Lifetime movies. This man rescued her. He was a good guy. Mick was just a player. Besides, she wanted him to make a move. Didn't she? Still...

"Nice place." He spoke, breaking the silence surrounding them.

She turned toward him, watching as his eyes roamed the living area. Her newly painted walls and sparking tiled floors. Her overstuffed white couch with the vivid floral throw pillows. He eyed the large-screen TV with evident appreciation. Then without another word, he turned toward her. His gaze settled on her face, moved down her neck, and stopped. "You're bleeding. You may have a piece of glass stuck in your shoulder. I better have a look."

"All right. Follow me." She led him down the hallway.

Once inside the brightly lit, marble-tiled bathroom, Rebecca did as he suggested and plopped herself down on the edge of the oversized garden tub.

"This may hurt a bit." His voice was low and throaty.

"It's okay." Her voice came out more like a squeak.

Rebecca swallowed and focused on the man who'd swept into her life tonight. She reached for a washcloth from the towel rack. For some reason, she felt the need to speak. "Thanks again for rescuing me."

"The least I could do for a beautiful woman." He smiled as he took the washcloth she offered. His fingers brushed gently over hers.

A sizzle of electricity ran up her arm from his touch. Rebecca shivered then shifted, leaning a little bit toward him. His fingers had barely moved across hers, but she reacted as if he touched a more secret spot.

Rebecca wanted to look away, but she couldn't help herself. The sensual way he gazed at her, his dark blue eyes drinking her in, even dressed in biker chick denim and leather, made her feel as if draped in silk and satin. Mick was the most incredible man she'd ever seen.

"That was quite a lousy experience for you tonight."

A forced smile tugged at her lips, and she nodded.

Mick brushed long strands of hair away from her wounded shoulder so he could doctor it. As he did, his face moved close to hers. Oh, God, this guy. Bad boy band guy or not, he sure brought out feelings she'd never had. Men never made her nervous until now. She rubbed her palms against her jeans and pulled in a breath.

"You ready, Sweetheart?"

The double entendre flooded heat into her veins as the loaded question ran through her. Oh, baby, I've been ready since the minute I saw you.

For the first time in her life, she wanted sex with a total stranger. But it was one thing to want it and still another for her to actually do it.

She winced as he lifted the material of her leather halter slightly to check her wound.

"Sorry."

"I'm fine." Rebecca licked her lips nervously.

Mick frowned. "Do you have tweezers and antiseptic?"

"In the drawer." She pointed toward the vanity.

His fingers touched her bare skin, and her heart raced. Gently, he pushed aside the strap on her top, and she squeezed her eyes shut as he did. "Ouch."

"Sorry." Again, he apologized.

"I'm okay. Really."

"Just another minute."

Rebecca nodded.

"Got it."

Her eyes opened to find him smiling at her. "Wow, it didn't hurt. Thank you, Mick."

"You're welcome."

Rebecca smiled. "You were very gentle."

"I had paramedic training. Briefly thought about being a fireman." He dabbed the antiseptic over the cut. "Sting?"

She flinched slightly under his touch. "It's good." The stuff stung like crazy, but she wasn't about to let him know. "Really? A fireman." Her curious nature peaked. "Then you decided to become a singer with a band?"

Mick shrugged. "Something like that." He flashed an amazing Brad Pitt type smile. "Bandages are?"

"Same drawer. You may have to dig around toward the back."

His eyebrows rose. Then finding what he needed, he moved back to her side and opened the bandage from its package.

"Your skin is soft," he murmured as he smoothed the bandage he'd skillfully placed over her wound. "You're a very lovely woman."

A moment of silence passed between them.

No doubt he'd used that line on several women before. Well, she wasn't going to fall for it but still…he was so darn attractive. She pulled in a deep breath.

Slowly his fingers moved up from her shoulder and trailed along her collar bone, then one finger dipped slightly toward the cleavage her low-cut blouse exposed. Her nipples tightened, and her belly tingled. She realized she was still holding her breath and slowly tried to breathe normally, which was extremely hard because she knew what his mind was picturing.

The two of them tangled together, hot and sweaty, on her bed.

She was picturing the same thing.

Only he was a man who played in a band. Entirely different from anyone she'd dated. Tonight, the entire biker bar experience had been for kicks, a chance to experience a different lifestyle. Rayna was the one looking for a man in Mo's, not her. Mick wasn't at all the type she could ever want. At least she didn't think he was what she wanted.

She was so confused.

And he was so close.

Desire rushed through her again. Mick made her feel alive and unique. But isn't that how all band guys make women feel? Making women swoon is part of the job. Rebecca swallowed hard. Heaven help her. Could she continue to keep up the Reb personality? She could almost hear her father's voice ringing in her ears, 'Rebecca, don't do anything to embarrass the family.'

Her throat tightened. Ha! That's a good one, she thought. I guess he's a 'do as I say, not as I do' father.

Her wild side bubbled to the surface. It doesn't matter if Mick's not my Mr. Right. He's hot, standing right here, and I don't have to please anyone but myself.

Mick's warm breath brushed her cheek. It would be too late if she didn't stop him right this minute. Okay, Reb, go with the moment. It's a game. Without another thought, she closed her eyes and whispered. "Kiss me, Mick."

His hand rose to cup her chin and gently tilted her head back.

Rebecca's mouth was a breath away from his when the wig she was wearing slid ungracefully from her head and landed in a heap inside the empty tub.

Mick's sharp intake of breath spoke volumes. Nope, he'd had no idea she was wearing a wig.

Crap. Her cheeks flooded pink with embarrassment and her hands flew to her face trying to stifle a burst of hysterical laughter. Talk about ruining the moment.

This was the first time Mick had a girl flip her wig over him. He blinked, glanced toward the hair in the tub, then back to meet her shaken gaze. "Uh, Reb, you're not a blonde. Got any more surprises for me?"

Color drained from her face as she turned her gaze toward the floor.

Mick groaned. Damn it. He hadn't meant to embarrass her. Unsure what to do, he freed the silky, light brown hair from the pins she used to keep her hair secured under the wig. His fingers threaded through the heavy curls. "Why the fake hair? You don't need it."

She shrugged and then nervously chewed her bottom lip.

Hair was not a topic Reb wanted to discuss, and he needed to change the subject, and quick. "So, tell me a little about yourself."

"Not much to tell." She shrugged again.

"I'll bet you have an interesting story."

She shook her head and mumbled something he couldn't understand.

He tried again. "Where do you work?"

Her perfectly arched brows lifted. "I recently accepted a position with attorney Paul Whittaker."

"I've heard of him." He'd heard of him all right. They'd played golf together more than once. In fact, Whittaker had sent a lot of business his way.

"What's your job title?"

"Um...er...no real title."

"No. Okay, so, what do you do there?"

"Um...Oh, just a little...er...um...this and that. Um...you know, answer the phone, file paperwork. I do lots of research." She cleared her throat. "Nothing fun."

"Well, that's a start. You can work your way up in the company." Wow. Reb was different. Most women he knew wouldn't stop talking about themselves. He was having a heck of a time getting her to open up. Maybe a compliment would help. "Have I mentioned you have lovely eyes?"

She blushed and glanced away, then turned back to him and spoke. "Mick, if I tell you something, will you promise not to be mad?" Her tone sounded severe.

This was a turn of events. What could Reb say that would cause him to be mad?

Curiosity triggered him to respond. "I'm listening."

She pursed her lips and then slowly nodded. "I'm not sure you truly want to know." She glanced down at her arms and began picking at the stones on her bracelet.

"Why wouldn't I want to know?"

"Fine. But you may not like what you hear."

He was starting to get a bit worried. She had a strange expression on her face as she continued to play with her bracelet. The only thing he could think of, off the top, was that maybe she was married. He glanced at her hands. No. No wedding ring. But she was wearing an expensive diamond bracelet. At least they looked like diamonds to him. She could be in a relationship.

Mick nodded, "Reb, tell me what's on your mind."

She lifted her smoky gaze to his, and he noticed how sky blue her eyes appeared in the bright light of the bathroom. "Truth is...I'm not exactly who you think I am." She frowned. "I've lived pretty much by my parent's rules." She glanced down momentarily, then looked up to face him. "I've attended the best schools. I followed in my father's footsteps. Entered the field of work expected from my parents."

Mick couldn't help but grin as he pondered her statement. "Sounds like you grew up with a wonderful family." Finally, he was getting her to talk to him.

"I suppose." She offered him a quivering smile. "Look, no offense." Her tone abruptly turned cold. "You've been nice to me tonight, bringing me home and all, but I have no plans to return to Mo's. And I certainly have no intention of becoming a band groupie." She tilted her head slightly. "Sorry to disappoint you."

Disappointment was the furthest thing from his mind. At this moment, he was more confused than anything else. All he'd expected was a chance to tell her how much he liked her, how pretty she was, and learn more about her. Not get a true confession. However, it was good news that she wasn't married. Mick breathed a sigh of relief and covered it by clearing his throat. "You haven't disappointed me."

"Oh, well, I was afraid…."

"Shh." He brushed a finger across her lips. "I don't want you to be afraid to talk to me."

"I am not afraid of you," she shot back.

"No?" He leaned closer to her angry but beautiful face. "That's good." His attention zeroed in on her gorgeous mouth, those full lips, all pink and pouty.

"Mick, you don't have to be nice to me. We're not at the bar."

"At the bar?" He frowned. "I'm not sure what you mean."

"Look. I know you were told to be friendly to me. You were instructed to come to our table and sing."

"Huh?" Oh, right. His boss had asked him to sing to her. "Yes but asking you to dance with me is not a requirement. And the sparks between us, they were real. You felt them too."

She flushed slightly and met his gaze. "I did, but...."

"Hey," he said softly. He looked into her eyes, trying to show Reb through them that he didn't want her to be a groupie. He wanted to get to know her better. One-on-one. "Reb, what's your deal? What are you looking for?"

She seemed surprised by his question. "I don't know." She shrugged, "I guess that's my problem."

She glanced toward the ceiling briefly and then down at the floor. As she did, her long brown hair fell over her face hiding what Mick knew were tears on the brink of spilling onto her cheeks. "All I know is that I want to break out of the traditional, proper behavior I've exhibited all my life. I need a new lifestyle. I want to live on the wild side."

Mick, indeed, was acquainted with those feelings. She was saying exactly what he felt before discovering the exhilaration of occasional nights with the band. Music had become his escape. He was always ready and willing when his friend, who owned Mo's bar, needed someone to fill in on stage at the last moment. But it was his damn lousy luck that he'd have to keep it a secret. She'd automatically dismiss him if he told her he was a tax attorney by day. To her, he'd be like every other guy she knew or ever dated.

He took a deep breath inhaling the intoxicating fragrance of her. Lavender and vanilla mingled together, heightening his desire. He felt almost dizzy, yet the strongest drink he'd had at Mo's was a couple of swigs of a lite beer. Before he took more time to think about his words, he blurted, "Well, I'm your answer." He gave a small laugh. "I live my life in the fast lane."

She giggled. The sound was so rich and sweet that she took his breath away.

He covered her hand with his and gave it a slight squeeze. "Reb, let me show you a different side of life."

Her smile wavered. "Look, Mick, I'm trying not to be rude, but" her voice dropped to a whisper, "you can't give me what I want." She appeared to regret her words the minute they left her mouth. Her lips pressed together in a tight line.

"You just told me you don't know what you want. Remember?"

She gave out a breathy little laugh. "Okay, I'll give you that one." She lowered her head, shielding her expression from him. "You sound like my friends. They're always telling me how I can't possibly know what I want if I don't give some different options a try. Actually, that's how I ended up at Mo's tonight." She rose from the tub's edge and slipped her arms around his neck.

Her eyes bored into his.

Trusting him.

"I'm very attracted to you. So, if I decide to let you show me your wild side of life, what would you want me to do?"

Mick stared into her baby blues wishing for the correct answer to give her. An emotion he hadn't felt for a long time began to build inside him. This woman was different, and he wanted her for more than one night. But would she want him if she knew he was a boring tax attorney? Most likely not. He'd be like every other guy she knew. So, to keep her in his life, he would need to lie. Would it be worth the chance to see where their relationship could go? He decided to find out before he changed his mind.

"This." He lowered his mouth to hers.

Chapter Four

Rebecca shivered as Mick's warm breath brushed her cheek. His lips remained close, and then he kissed her again. Sweet and smooth as a glass of expensive whiskey. As the pressure on her mouth increased, her eyes slowly closed, and her lips parted enough to let his tongue slip inside. Rebecca returned his kiss, exploring his mouth as he explored hers. The sensation of their lips and tongues moving together in a slow seductive dance. Their sensual kisses continued until her knees buckled, and she had to hold on tight to his shoulders to keep from sinking to the bathroom floor in a melted puddle.

Wrapped in his safe and secure arms, Rebecca realized she was about to do something the rational old Rebecca vowed she'd never let happen. Warning bells rang in her ears. How often had she been told, never sex on a first date? If you give it away too easily, you'll never hear from him again. Did she even want to hear from him again? Would a woman like Reb care? No.

Absolutely Rebecca did.

Of course, she reminded herself, this wasn't an actual date. She'd only let Mick give her a ride home from an unfamiliar biker bar. Not her regular hangout at the Ritz, where at least one of her friends could vouch for a guy's integrity, or lack of it, if she asked. But certainly, a lot of the regulars at Mo's knew Mick. But there'd been no time to ask about him before the fight broke out, and he'd swept her out of harm's way. If she'd asked, what would she have heard? Would she have been warned to watch her heart? What if she asked if he often picked up women? Oh, what a silly question. He was a band guy. Of course, he did, most likely every night.

Didn't he?

Her mind bounced all over the place.

Plus, she'd lied to him. Well, not an actual lie, and she'd only left out a detail or two. Still, not being truthful went against everything she believed. But she hadn't been able to tell him about the prestigious job she'd accepted right out of law school, and she wasn't sure why. Maybe she didn't want to explain why she was play-acting in a biker bar. Oh, good heavens, what a muddle.

Breaking their kiss enough to speak, Mick breathed the words into her ear, sending tremors through her body, "Let's go into another room."

Her heart skipped a beat, and his meaning was loud and clear. All Rebecca's internal alarms sounded again. She realized she wasn't in any physical danger, only that she might make a mistake and have regrets in the morning.

What should she do?

"If you'd rather not, Reb, if your shoulder hurts, tell me. I'll go."

Shoulder? Oh, yeah, she'd forgotten about the glass embedded in her shoulder earlier. "I'm not in any pain." But she certainly was tingling. Everywhere.

The air around them sizzled with sexual tension.

She tilted her head to better look at his handsome features as she skimmed her fingers over his well-muscled shoulders and down his strong arms. His dark blue eyes glazed with passion making her feel like she was the most beautiful woman he'd ever seen.

Time to decide.

Who was she kidding? She already knew the answer, even if it would only be for one night. She'd own it. She'd live for the moment. And right at this moment, as the 'new' Rebecca, she couldn't think of a better idea than getting naked and crawling into her bed with Mick.

Drawing a slow, steady breath, she reached for his hand and led him out of the brightly lit bathroom.

#

Mick left the decision entirely up to Reb. He certainly didn't want her to think he only rescued her from the bar to get laid. After getting her safely home, he'd accepted her invitation to come inside, hoping to get to know her better. Plus, he wanted to ensure she hadn't hurt herself during the bar brawl. He had every intention of asking her on a future date, and it had nothing to do with whether she slept with him tonight.

Mick knew he was moving a bit too fast, but the way he felt right now, he hoped, no, prayed, she wanted him as much as he wanted her. He almost whooped with joy when she took his hand and headed out of the bathroom. With his fingers linked with hers, he followed her down the hallway until she stopped and turned to him, eyes glimmering in the soft light inside the bedroom. "I don't do casual sex, Mick."

Mick pulled in a breath. He hadn't expected her to say this.

"I mean, I'm not asking you to commit to anything. I am just saying…."

He lifted her hand to his lips and gently brushed a kiss across each finger. "Baby, nothing about tonight is going to be casual."

Her smile widened, and a mischievous glint appeared in her eyes. Pulling her hand away, she backed toward the bedroom.

There was no mistaking her intentions. Completely caught in the moment, Mick followed her into the dimly lit room.

Still smiling, she kicked off her high heels, then unzipped her skin-tight jeans. As she shimmied out of them, he watched, knowing he had a stupid grin plastered across his face, but he couldn't help it. His eyes seemed glued to her.

He focused on her long, bare legs and his breathing grew shallow. Slowly his gaze moved upward to her sexy black panties, which were merely a strip of lace, but he noticed the colors above her hip bone as she slid them down and tossed them aside.

A tattoo. Reb had a tattoo. Delicate swirls of blues and greens, perfectly designed into the shape of a butterfly. His hand reached out and skimmed one finger along the outline of the wings. Her skin felt so soft, so smooth.

She took a step back, unfastened her halter top then slowly let it slide off her shoulders. Mick held his breath. She wasn't wearing a bra, and he'd suspected she wasn't but hadn't been sure until now.

"Beautiful." Like the words he sang to her on the dance floor, she was beautiful tonight. He ran his gaze over her trim body as she stood completely naked. Her long wavy hair, her hair, not the wig she'd worn earlier, her gorgeous breasts with the nipples taunt and rosy, the curve of her slim waist. "You are gorgeous."

"Take off your clothes, Mick."

Before he could answer, she pushed off his vest, and her fingers began twisting the fabric of his T-shirt.

When he slid it over his head and flung it to the nearest chair, she moved closer and placed her lips on his bare chest. It was just the gentlest kiss, brief and swift. "Mmm," he moaned as her hands reached between them to unfasten his 501's. Then her hands slid away, and she stepped back slightly to watch while he hastily undressed.

They stood face to face for a brief minute, seeming to enjoy each other's nakedness. A surge of lust pounded through his veins. Finally, Mick stepped forward and placed both hands on her hips, holding her like that for a second, then pulled her body close. Her firm breasts rubbing against his skin caused beads of perspiration to pop across his forehead. Slowly his fingers moved along her backbone, and a wave of excitement flooded him when she shivered under his touch. Her arms reached up and folded around his neck.

Holding each other tightly, their bodies began to sway together in a slow dance. Mick hummed softly into her ear as he moved her toward the bed. When she reached the edge of the mattress, she let herself fall backward, pulling him along.

Landing on her, he slid one leg between hers before covering her mouth with a deep, passionate kiss.

He broke their kiss and smiled down at her. "You are a gorgeous woman, Reb." He kissed her again, slowly moving lower to her cheek and neck.

"Mick...wait!"

"Wait?" Mick squeezed his eyes closed and prayed for the restraint to be able to stop. "Do you want me to quit?"

"I...I...your last name. What's your last name?"

"Harris. It's Harris. Mick Harris."

Taking hold of his hair, she pulled his head close to her lips, her breath warm on his face. "Kiss me, Mick Harris."

And he did. Long and hard.

Breaking the kiss, he teased her lips with his tongue, and she responded by digging her nails into his shoulders. Gently, he kissed her again, wanting to share this intoxicating pleasure of the two of them discovering one another with powerful ease, knowing he had all night.

He closed his eyes, let his other senses sharpen, and indulged all her feelings so yielding in his arms. Everything felt right, as if she'd always belonged with him. She did, Mick knew, and he belonged with her, gliding in this world of warm kisses and pleasure. Such pleasure. This is what he'd been waiting for all his life.

For tonight.

For her.

"Reb." He whispered, loving the sound of her name on his lips. "I want you."

She exhaled a sound of agreement and lifted her hips to his, setting off another surge of passion even stronger than before. He felt it rise between them. He wanted to take it slow, but as he rubbed against her, teasing her with the promise of entry, she wrapped her legs around his hips, pulling him in. Unable to help himself, he entered her with one massive thrust. Oh, yes, she was tight and welcoming, everything he'd hoped she'd be, so warm and wet.

Mick, determined to take it slow, focused on his pace as they rocked into one another, her hips dancing with his movements while exchanging deep kisses and gentle touches. All the while, his mind spun with sexy, crazy ideas he wanted to do with her.

His imagination didn't fully serve him. At some point during the night, they'd gone from the bed to the floor, to a shower, then back on the bed again. And he vaguely remembered them having sex on the kitchen counter when he went to get a glass of water, and, damn, what that girl did to him with ice cubes. Not to mention when she chased after him armed with her salad tongs. He'd never laughed so much while having sex. Mick knew without a doubt this woman was different from anyone he'd known before, and his life would never be the same.

But the Mick she knew was a phony. What if she knew the honest Mick?

He pushed the thought from his mind and reached for her again.

Gently feathering a kiss to her forehead, he rolled onto his back and nestled her under his arm. As they lay peacefully, with their arms wrapped around each other and one of Reb's long, slender legs draped over his, he drifted to sleep.

Beep! Beep!

It seemed he'd only closed his eyes when the high-pitched noise assaulted his ears.

Beep! Beep! Beep!

"What's happening?" His throat felt like someone stuffed it with cotton balls.

"My alarm. I'm turning it off."

When the irritating sound stopped, he slid his arm around her, pulling her back to him. "Good morning, beautiful. How'd you sleep?"

"Never better," she whispered. "All glorious half hour of it."

Mick smiled.

The early morning sunlight peeking through the bedroom window highlighted her hair as it cascaded over her creamy shoulders. At this moment, he couldn't remember ever waking up to a vision more beautiful.

"Reb, tell me your fantasies. I want to fulfill each one for you." He kissed her neck, her cheek, and the corner of her mouth. "I'll do whatever you want. Tell me what will make you happy." He meant every word he spoke.

"I don't know, Mick. I only know I want excitement. I want to be someone different. Someone wild."

"I'll be glad to show you more of the wild side, starting in…oh, say, two minutes." He took her hand and slid it under the covers to touch him. "See what you're doing to me?"

She laughed and pulled her hand away. "Well, that's wonderful, but I have a job, and I need to get going." She kissed his cheek, scooted off the bed, and disappeared into the bathroom.

Mick let out a low laugh and ran his hand through his disheveled hair. He hated to leave but figured it was time for him to get going. He had a long, hectic day ahead of him with a client arriving early. He needed to go home, shower, and change into different clothes. He swung his legs over the side of the bed and rose to his feet. "Hey, I have an idea. We'll have dinner tonight, and you can make me a list."

She cracked the bathroom door and peeked out. "A list?" Her brows scrunched.

"Yep." He grabbed his shirt from the chair and shook it, hoping to remove some of the wrinkles. "A list of all the things you'd like to try."

"You mean like skydiving?"

"If that's your wish. Of course, I'm hoping there are some sexual fantasies on it."

"We'll see about a list, but dinner sounds fine." She closed the bathroom door again.

Typically, when he asked a client for a list, he'd offer them a pen. Instinctively he reached for the one inside the pocket of his vest. Then, he remembered it had his name and logo on it and caught himself. Mick groaned and rubbed a hand over his face. He wasn't working in his office. He was in Reb's bedroom. The night with her had been perfect. Such a part of him now. And he planned to take particular joy in making every one of her fantasies come true.

But as he tugged on his jeans, the scary thought nagged him. How long could he go without telling her the truth about who he was, and when he did, what would she say?

Chapter Five

Rebecca tried to convince herself a biker bar musician was not someone to allow into her heart. She and Mick couldn't be in a long-term relationship; they were too different, and each had entirely different goals. She didn't know his aspirations, but she knew hers didn't include a biker bar musician. Oh, sure, right now, she wanted some fun and excitement, but in the long run, whatever her true persona turned out to be, some things wouldn't change. She'd always need security and stability in her life, and she wouldn't get those from a bad-boy musician. What she'd get was her heart broken.

So why was she having such a hard time not thinking about him? And why had she agreed to dinner? He'd promised to keep it casual and bring the food, but her better judgment knew it wasn't a good idea. Mick was too charming, too sexy, too, oh goodness, to everything.

Finally, she sighed, closed the open file on her desk, and leaned back into her plush leather chair. She glanced around her prestigious office at Whitaker Law Firm. She'd accepted the position as an assistant attorney right out of law school. Thanks to her father, the job came without the usual networking, mailing out resumes, or starting from the bottom doing pro bono work. Coming from a prominent political family did have its advantages. She was grateful for that much, and Whitaker Law was the perfect workplace. At least for now.

She took in her surroundings. The high-rise building in downtown Phoenix had been recently remodeled to reflect Mr. Whitaker's excellent taste. She smiled approvingly. On one side of her seventh-floor office space, built-in bookshelves displayed all her leather-bound law books. Behind her desk hung an oil painting of a sailboat gliding across crystal clear waters. She had bought the picture while on a family vacation in Cabo. She frowned. Those days were probably over now that her father…Oh, stop it. Don't let your mind go there again.

She abruptly stood and moved toward the floor-to-ceiling window. Pulling in a deep cleansing breath, she gazed out to watch how the noonday sunshine sparkled rainbow colors off the water flowing from the fountain below. Looking through this window, enjoying the fountain, and surrounding landscape, for some reason, always calmed her.

Her parents had raised her to fit into this world, but it didn't feel especially good right now. She wasn't going to think about her parents and what they wanted for her anymore today. So, what should she think about instead?

Mick instantly popped into her mind...again.

She let her thoughts wander back to last night. Mick's lean body, soul-piercing eyes, warm breath on her skin, how they'd done crazy things she'd never considered. Who knew you could have so much fun with ice cubes, a shower massager, scarves, piles of pillows, and salad tongs? She laughed softly out loud. Then, she remembered his voice. How the words Mick sang to her as they danced at Mo's had touched each nerve ending of her body.

Her nipples tightened, and her stomach fluttered. She swayed a bit and smiled. If nothing else, she'd stepped out of her world to have one night with a bad boy biker in a band. Indeed, something she never expected, and he had been phenomenal. But she hadn't been candid with him. Would it have mattered to him if she had?

A light tapping jarred her back to the present. She turned to find Trisha standing in the open doorway. "Hi." Her friend smiled and then held up a white paper sack. "I brought lunch."

What a fantastic surprise. Rebecca waved her in. "Your timing is perfect. I'm starving."

Trisha stepped into the office and placed the bag from the downtown deli onto Rebecca's desk. "I know you like tuna salad."

"Love it," Rebecca answered, motioning for Trisha to scoot a chair closer.

Dressed in a bright-colored maxi dress of corals and greens that complimented her olive complexion, her dark hair falling in loose waves to her shoulders, Trisha radiated confidence. Rebecca couldn't help but admire her friend's style. This woman knew exactly who she was and had no problem letting everyone see the authentic Trisha. She also remembered Rebecca carried a heavy workload and rarely left the office for lunch.

Rebecca cleared her workspace as Trisha retrieved two sandwiches and two bottles of sparkling water from the bag. "One's on wheat, and one's on rye. Take your pick."

"Wheat."

Trisha handed Rebecca the chosen sandwich, a napkin, and one of the bottled waters.

Rebecca unwrapped hers, then immediately lifted the top half of the wheat roll and removed an onion slice. "Did you bring pickles?"

"Of course." Trisha placed a small container between them.

They sat across from each other, chatting while savoring the meal, and neither was saying anything of importance. Finally, Trisha asked, "So, tell me what happened last night." Her eyes gleamed with curiosity as she stared over the last bite of her tuna on rye.

"I should be asking you what happened after I left. Did you all go straight home?"

"Don't try to change the subject. First you."

Glancing toward the door to ensure it was closed, Rebecca leaned forward and whispered, "I had sex with him."

"You what?"

"We had sex. I did it with the band guy."

"Oh, my god!" Realizing she'd yelled, Trisha lowered her voice and continued, "And I'm guessing he was fantastic." She gave a knowing lift of her eyebrows.

Rebecca smiled. "Let's just say he's a man who knows how to make a woman happy." She burst into a fit of laughter. "Yes, it was fantastic. The sexiest night of my life."

"Well, hot damn! I'm proud of you."

"But, Trisha, a guy who plays in a band at a biker bar." She shrugged. "You know that's not what I'm looking for."

Trisha shook her head. "You don't know what you're looking for, Rebecca. Besides, I feel there's more to Mick than meets the eye."

"Maybe." She twisted off the cap on the water bottle. "I wonder how a biker-bar band guy can be so incredibly thoughtful. So responsive. So, understanding of my desire to show up at work on time—the last thing I'd expect from such a man."

"You must be kidding? Regardless of the venue, anyone who plays in a band understands the importance of punctuality."

The intercom buzzed. Rebecca waved a hand toward Trisha, signaling she needed to answer it. "Yes?"

The office receptionist said in her usual matter-of-fact voice. "Rebecca, Miss Summers from channel 10 TV is on the line. She'd like to interview you at your earliest convenience."

Rebecca knew that meant only one thing. Miss Summers wanted to discover how her father's transgressions affected her, her family, and his career. "Tell her I'm unavailable."

"I can do that." The voice on the other end added, "If you're sure."

"Oh, never mind. Let her know I'm free this afternoon at three." Rebecca punched the button so hard that the intercom almost fell off the desk. She bit back a curse.

Trisha stood and hastily gathered the leftovers from their lunch. As she stuffed the finished items into the trash, she asked, "You'll be okay?"

"Of course." She took a steadying breath. "I'm fine. I'm, oh, I don't know what I am."

"Hey, none of this is your fault. It's your father's mess. Let him deal with it."

Rebecca sank deeper in her chair and crossed her legs. "You're right. I know you're right. It's just, well, it's not that simple."

"Nothing is ever simple." Trisha glanced at her watch. "Hey, I gotta run. I have an appointment with a client at two o'clock." She stepped around the desk to hug Rebecca. "As for Mick, don't do anything hasty. He could be your Mr. Right."

"I doubt it. Anyway, I'm not looking at Mick through rose-colored glasses.

"Do you want to go out later and talk some more? I can check with Scarlett and Rayna. They can meet us at the Ritz."

"Thanks for the offer but not tonight. Mick is coming for dinner."

"Dinner? An actual date. It sounds like you two are moving toward a relationship."

"No." her voice came out sharper than she intended. "I mean, it's a casual dinner. Mick's picking up pizza. Oh, but get this. He told me to make a list."

"List? What kind of list?"

"A list of things I want to do, and I think he was referring to sex."

"Really." Trisha gave her a curious look. "What's on it so far?"

"Nothing."

"Nothing? Huh." She tilted her head. "I bet you can think of plenty of things." Trisha stood, pushed her chair back from the desk waved goodbye as she headed for the door.

Rebecca waved back. "Maybe," she muttered as her friend exited the office.

She picked up the file she was working on earlier, then slammed it shut again. She glanced over to the piece of paper labeled List. Resting her head on her left hand, she absentmindedly tapped on the blank sheet with her right finger. Whenever she tried to think of outrageous activities or exciting places to have sex, all that came to mind was an ordinary evening at home. Just the two of them. No special costumes. No erotic toys. Just her and Mick and her 300-thread-count sheets.

She leaned her forehead into her hands and groaned. Still slumped over her desk, she whispered, "So, what would Reb put on a list?"

After staring at the blank sheet for several minutes with no ideas popping into her mind, she opened the top drawer of her desk and slid the paper inside. Unfortunately, Rebecca didn't have all day to sit around thinking about a silly list. She had a full day of research for Mr. Whitaker's upcoming trial, and he'd be expecting her report soon. But as her eyes fixed on her computer, her musings returned to her hopeful personality adjustment.

What would happen if she allowed her rebel personality to take over? Would she decide to quit her job? She loved her promising law career, but the new rebel-hearted Reb would probably rather be a pole dancer.

Or a barrel racer. Or something even wilder.

The ridiculous ideas made her smile. Then sucking in a deep breath, Rebecca turned on her computer and returned to work.

Chapter Six

They had agreed to meet at seven o'clock for a casual dinner. Mick was picking up a pizza on his way over, and Rebecca was making a salad and supplying the wine. Both of her contributions were ready and chilling in the fridge. She'd taken a quick shower, pulled on her favorite jeans, and after changing tops three times, decided on a comfortable T-shirt.

When her hair fell into perfect waves without much effort, she stared into the bathroom mirror at her image. "At least something is going in my favor today."

Rebecca had been unable to shake off the chill of the interview earlier this afternoon. It was supposed to be about a current client her office was defending, but as she had anticipated it would happen, the reporter brought up her father and his wrongdoings. She thought she was ready for the questions, but as it turned out, the reporter had been brutal. She handled it as best she could, but it still cut to the bone defending her father's actions on live television. It seemed like she had backstabbed her mother and went against her beliefs.

Ridiculous, of course, she had told herself. She had done exactly what was expected of her. After all, she followed her mother's instructions. Appearances were always the most important she'd said. If her father betrayed his family, lived a lie, and kept another woman on the side while serving his term as a state senator, she was to act as if everything was simply okay.

Yeah. Right. It would never be fine as far as Rebecca was concerned. Twisting the truth, for whatever reason, went against every fiber of her being. That was what made becoming an attorney as a career choice so attractive. Her goal was to bring out the truth. Protect the innocent and stand up for people being taken advantage of by con artists and scammers. It was about helping people who needed help. And, yet, she'd held back facts about herself from Mick. What did that say about herself?

A soft tapping brought her back to the present, right on time. Checking her reflection in the mirror, she turned and headed for the front door. Taking a calming, deep breath, she turned the knob, but not before wondering how Mick had dressed for their evening.

He looked even better than she remembered, sexy and a little disheveled. His dark hair fell across his forehead, and his clean-shaven face expressed an appealing smile. No doubt about it, this man cleaned up nicely and was dangerously hot.

"Hi."

"Hi," he answered with a smooth, velvet voice. "Pizza and wings are coming soon. I ordered delivery." He turned his head toward the Harley parked in her driveway. "Wasn't sure I could get the food here intact."

Rebecca's tummy did a little flip-flop, not in anticipation of pizza. She remembered how it felt to be pressed against his muscular back, the wind blowing across her face, and it had been exhilarating. "Good idea."

Drawing a slow, steady breath, she stepped back and motioned for him to enter.

"I brought something for you." A cute grin tugged at the corners of his mouth as he held up the handbag she'd left at Mo's.

"Thank you." She grabbed the purse. "I didn't expect to see this again. A Coach and a favorite of mine."

"Not a problem. Happy to make you smile."

Rebecca still couldn't believe she was so attracted to him, but seriously, why wouldn't she be? He was beyond a good-looking man. And right now, Mick was precisely who she needed, someone to take her mind off her family problems and career stress. Not to mention the horrible interview she'd endured this afternoon. Her stomach tightened with the memory. She'd never forget how awful the reporter had made her feel.

Now she had to remember to keep guard on her heart. There will be no commitment between us. She reminded herself. We're a casual friendship with benefits—just a good time.

She tossed the handbag into a nearby chair. "Thirsty? I have wine."

"Sounds nice."

Moving into the kitchen, Rebecca set two crystal glasses on the counter and then turned to the fridge to retrieve the chilled bottle.

"Here, let me open that," he offered as he stepped closer, reaching to take the wine from her hand.

The nearness of his body rushed goosebumps across her skin. "Thank you." She smiled. While he poured, she busied herself, tossing the salad and filling two glass bowls with the garden greens. "I have both ranch and a zesty Italian dressing. Take your pick."

"Zesty."

She nodded. "Perfect."

He tilted his head and raised an eyebrow flirtatiously.

Rebecca laughed and placed both bottles of salad dressing on the counter. "I like ranch with pizza." Looking up, she met his gaze. He'd moved closer to hand her a glass of wine. They were only two steps from each other now. Suddenly self-conscious, she noticed the twinkle in his eyes. Did he remember last night? She did. He took a step nearer and gently ran his fingers along her cheek. Her skin flushed under his touch, and every one of her senses ignited.

"Reb," he whispered as his lips almost met hers.

"Mmm," was all she could manage.

The doorbell rang. At the sound, she startled, almost spilling wine down the front of her shirt. Luckily, only a few drops were splashed across the counter.

"Sounds like the dinner bell," he announced. Smiling, he headed toward the front door.

She set down the wine glass with a shaky hand and blew out a steadying breath. Truly a saved-by-the-bell moment, she thought, as she struggled to regain her composure.

A few minutes later, she deeply inhaled as she lifted the cardboard box lid. The spicy aroma of the pizza rushed through her making her tummy growl. She filled their plates with two generous slices, several hot chicken wings, and a bowl of fresh, tossed green salad.

Once seated, Rebecca wasted no time. Without considering her manners, she dipped her pizza slice into her ranch dressing, then stuffed a generous bite into her mouth. Her taste buds ignited with the perfect combination of salty, spicy pepperoni and rich tomato sauce, covered with melting mozzarella cheese, and dripping with cool, creamy ranch dressing. Delicious. Happily chewing, she glanced toward Mick and caught him staring. She tried to hide her embarrassment by covering her mouth with her free hand.

"You got sauce on your chin," he said jokingly, reaching over and wiping her face with his napkin.

"Sorry but eating pizza and wings like a lady is hard. Just turn away." She reached for a wing. "These look delicious."

"I've always had a thing for a woman who enjoys her food." He smiled and held up his glass.

"Yeah, well, as I said, you better look away because I'm going to enjoy this meal." She returned the wing to her plate, picked up her wine, and raised it to his, "To a wonderful dinner."

He nodded and leaned closer. "And a beautiful woman."

The crystal glasses clinked lightly.

# # #

Mick couldn't stop staring. In her cute T-shirt, the blue color matching her eyes, her hair falling in soft waves over her shoulders, and wearing only enough lipstick to make her lips look even more kissable, Reb was

73

beautiful. His selfish inner demon surfaced. He needed to tell her the truth. But when he did, would she dismiss him afterward? He couldn't stand the thought of never seeing her again. Still, he couldn't keep lying.

He'd have to figure out a way to confess who he was, and he would as soon as the time was right. When that time would be, he had no idea. He just knew, for now, he'd need to wait a bit longer. He was falling hard for this woman and needed to make her care about him enough to understand his logic when he told her the truth.

"This was nice," she said as she picked up their plates. Mick watched her intently as she moved around the kitchen, placing their dirty dishes and silverware into the dishwasher.

He gathered the empty pizza and wings boxes, dropped them into the trash, then returned to the table and refilled both wine glasses. When the kitchen was cleaned to Rebecca's satisfaction, she sat next to him, picked up her glass, and took a sip. "Good wine."

"Reb?" he leaned closer and tried to push all the negative thoughts from his mind. "How's your list coming along?"

She shrugged. "Actually, I haven't started it."

He stared at her momentarily, then had a sudden thought. "No worries." A slow smile spread across his lips. "I can think of something you might like."

"You can?" She asked as her eyes widened.

"Come on." He reached for her hand and pulled her to her feet.

"What are we doing?"

"You'll see. Bring your wine." He wasn't sure why this idea popped into his head, but it seemed like something wild that Reb wouldn't have done before. At least he hoped she would like it and not be offended. He led her toward the back door.

They stepped outside without turning on the overhead patio light, paused, and instantly the sweet smells of honeysuckle and night-blooming star jasmine greeted them. A large lemon tree off the side of the patio bursting with fragrant flowering blooms filled the air. A cool breeze, kicked up from the overhead circling fan, added to the ambiance of the romantic setting.

Mick had noticed the chaise lounge chairs on the patio yesterday and was impressed by how nice her backyard looked. Tonight, as he stepped outside, he was overcome with more appreciation. Even though the area was small, it was impeccably manicured and only lit by the low-level lighting along the back wall—the perfect setting for his plan.

Motioning for Reb to sit, he took his phone and opened an app to romantic background music. Soon soft melody tones began to stream a pulsing beat to the otherwise quiet evening.

She lowered herself into the lounge chair and tilted her head, giving him a questioning look.

He smiled, knelt beside her, and set his drink on the concrete. Then he took her glass and placed it near his, close enough to easily reach but far away enough not to be knocked over. He didn't want broken glass scattered on her patio.

Leaning closer, he saw her smile slightly just before he gently brushed a kiss across her cheek. Then move to her lips. Their kiss continued as he made tender love to her mouth. He'd make this night all for her, slow and easy. Mick realized he was falling in love for the first time.

Gently his hand slipped under her T-shirt and touched her smooth skin. He felt her slightly quiver beneath his fingertips, urging him to move upward and cup one breast. Beneath the sheer fabric of her bra, her nipple hardened.

Mick broke their kiss, then lowered his hand to the bottom edge of her shirt and slowly pushed it upward. "Let's take this off."

She leaned forward and let him slide the soft material over her head. A low moan escaped him as he reached around and unfastened her bra. As both straps fell off her shoulders, Mick carefully removed the lacy fabric and tossed it along with her shirt behind the chair.

"Reb, you're so beautiful," he whispered. She gave a reply by arching upward, offering herself to him. He bent forward and kissed the curve of her breast, then slid his tongue over her hardened nipple.

"Is this wild enough for you, baby?" he spoke softly before closing his mouth over the firm bud and sucking deep. He slowly worked on each breast from one to the other until he heard her whispering how much she wanted him. Smiling to himself, he began inching his way down from her breasts to her midriff, then lower to tenderly kiss her above the button of her jeans.

"Mick." Her voice sounded nervous.

He glanced up and met her smoldering gaze. "Would you rather not?"

"This is perfect," she answered softly. "Sex outside with all the stars watching. Very exciting." She unzipped her jeans and pushed them down over her hips. "Yes. Let's be wild."

His answer was to slip his hand under her lace panties. Pushing the material aside, he lowered his mouth and ran his tongue over her delicate, sensitive flesh.

Reb's soft gasps of delight told him she approved.

"Oh, Mick, you're making me crazy," she whispered.

He continued without pausing until after she offered an ecstatic moan to the twinkling stars and slice of the moon shining vibrantly overhead.

Chapter Seven

What a way to start a Monday. Rebecca stepped inside her father's business office and watched the man communicate on his phone. His words flowed from his mouth like sweet pancake syrup. She wondered what would have happened if she'd refused to take his phone call earlier. What if she'd given him a flat no when he invited her to meet him at his office? Would it have made her feel better? Most likely not, so she'd agreed to his request.

She gritted her teeth as her father caught her eye and smiled. He cupped his hand over the phone. "One minute," he whispered while holding up his index finger.

The feeling swept over Rebecca again, the one where she felt as if she might explode. Sometimes the emotion made her want to throw her shoe against the wall, but most times, she'd choose to stand under a hot shower and let the tears flow.

Thank goodness she had her friends, Rayna, Scarlett, and Trisha. They stood by her side, giving support through the entire mess of her parents' public breakup. They also came up with trying on new personalities at different bars. Yeah, her girlfriends got creative at times.

They'd said it was the perfect diversion from her problems, but now she wasn't so sure. Maybe all her role-playing had done was create an entirely new issue. She'd met Mick and hid her true self. Now, it was becoming harder and harder to bring up the subject. She could blurt out. Hey, by the way, I'm Rebecca Prentice, Senator Prentice's daughter. And I'm also not a secretary. I'm an assistant attorney with the Whittaker Law Group.

But what if she told him and their relationship changed? Did she want that? She enjoyed being Reb, the wild woman who spoke her mind without worrying if it was politically correct. She could be reckless with Mick, someone without a care in the world. Oh, it wasn't realistic, but it was nice to block out all the stress of the day and be happy.

"Okay!" her father said jubilantly, interrupting her thoughts as he placed the receiver back into its cradle. Moving from his desk, he crossed the room quickly and draped an arm around her shoulder, pulling her close.

Immediately Rebecca was enveloped by the scents linked with her youth. Leather, sandalwood, the slightest hint of vanilla. She leaned into the familiar smells. Her eyes closed, remembering the past and the happier days. How could things have gone so wrong? She'd thought she had the perfect family.

Straightening her back, she pulled away and turned her head so he couldn't see the tears forming. She refused to let him see her cry.

He didn't seem to notice she was upset. Instead, he headed toward the doorway and cheerfully asked, "What do you say we grab some lunch and talk?"

Seriously. Dad wants to have lunch. Of course, he wants to look good to the public. Keep up appearances for the constituents.

"I don't have time today, Dad." Besides, the way her emotions were messing with her stomach, there was no way she could choke down any food.

"I understand, but it's important." His steel-blue eyes drilled into hers as he added, "I have a little surprise for you." He tilted his head. "Please."

Rebecca knew her father. He wouldn't let her off easy, and he'd keep bugging her, so she may as well get it over with and hear him out. She rolled her eyes. "Fine. Let's go."

They didn't speak during the elevator ride down to the main floor, then continued in silence as they crossed the street and headed toward their favorite dining establishment. The Ritz was already filling up with the lunch crowd when they stepped through the door.

"Ah, good. I see she's here." Her father pointed toward his usual table, a big smile plastered across his face.

Rebecca glanced toward the direction her father waved. Her eyes widened. I don't believe it, she thought. Sitting there casually sipping from a champagne flute was her mother. Upon seeing them, Olivia smiled brightly.

"Come on, darling, let's join your mother."

Before Rebecca had time to respond, her father ushered her to the table.

Once seated, a server appeared. Instantly recognizing them, she spoke, "Senator Prentice and Rebecca, wonderful to see you."

"It's nice to be here," Rebecca's father replied.

"Olivia and I have been having a nice chat." She and Olivia exchanged smiles. "What may I get for you today?" she asked.

"What's your special?" Olivia asked.

"Salmon salad, grilled, with an orange zest and balsamic vinaigrette glaze."

"Sounds delightful. I'll have that and another one of these." Olivia held up her glass.

"Rebecca?" The server looked at her, pen in hand, ready to write her order.

"Whatever mom's having." She still wasn't hungry. "White wine."

Her father ordered quickly. His usual medium-rare steak sandwich, side of fries, and his favorite cocktail, an Old Fashioned.

Her father began to speak as soon as the server left to place their order. "Rebecca, your mother, and I want to thank you for joining us. We've missed spending time together."

Not my fault, she wanted to say, but instead, she held her tongue. Taking a steadying breath, she smiled sweetly and nodded. She had no idea what was happening here today, but whatever it was, it was sure peculiar. Did her father think the three of them could eat a meal together like everything was okay? And what was up with her mother? How could she sit next to him like an everyday family luncheon? Rebecca shook her head. These two have some serious issues.

Their drinks arrived promptly, and Rebecca realized a glass of wine was an excellent idea. It tasted good. And much to her surprise made the thought of food sound appealing.

Her father took a long sip of his drink. "Ah, the bourbon here never disappoints."

Rebecca made quick eye contact with her mother, trying to get her reaction to what was happening. Mom only acknowledged her with a nod and a sweet smile.

Her father flexed his hands together as if preparing to make a statement before the council. "Rebecca, I suppose you're wondering what's happening here."

"That's for sure." Rebecca's gaze darted toward her mother again, then back to her father. "I am confused. Care to enlighten me?"

"Let me tell you a little story, honey."

Oh, Lord. Dad and his stories. Not needed right now, she thought.

"When your mom and I met, I knew it was our destiny to be together."

Olivia pushed back her salad and jumped into the conversation. "Marriage is more than passion and desire, but somehow, we let our essential bond fall apart."

"I was too busy to notice how we drifted away from each other," her father added. "Sure, your mom knew how important my work was to me, and, God love her, Olivia never protested the long hours I worked. However, I let my career become all-consuming."

He let out a sigh. "I wanted the best for my family, and I thought money was the way to prove it. At the time, I didn't realize Olivia had stopped talking to me. Our family functions and extravagant parties didn't compensate for our unspoken problems."

Olivia leaned closer and lowered her voice. "Eventually, we both looked for what was missing."

What was happening? Rebecca shook her head in disbelief. She must have misunderstood what her mother said. "What are you saying? Mom?"

"Yes, darling. I looked for happiness elsewhere as well."

"How did I not know this?" Rebecca shook her head and glared at her mother. "I would have known."

"Oh, no, that's just it, honey." Her mother met her stare. "We didn't want you to know. We did everything possible to protect you."

"This is plain crazy," Rebecca fumed. "I thought our life was perfect."

"Our life was perfect," her father declared. "Your mother and I weren't perfect." He shrugged his shoulders and drained the last of his drink. "We messed up. But we realize now that what we want is each other. We want to start over, to make things right this time. We aren't getting a divorce."

"Seriously?" After what you did to mom, she's forgiving you?"

"I am, dear. And bless your father's, generous heart. He's forgiving me as well."

"This is messed up." Rebecca's gaze skated from her mother to her father, then back to her mother. "Are you sure, mom? He lied to you. To both of us."

"I wasn't an angel myself. I never had an actual affair, but I had dinner dates. I attended parties with men friends on occasion."

"Still, that's different from what dad did to you."

"There's no other woman for me, Rebecca. I love your mother."

Rebecca rolled her eyes upward, then shook her head. "Well, what about the other woman, Dad? What about, oh, what's her name? Sandra or Susan?"

"Sophie," he told her. "She's out of my life now for good."

"Oh, right. I hear that daily in court," she responded. "Mom, you believe him?"

Her mother didn't hesitate. "I do."

"What about all the publicity? The newspaper writeups, and the tv reporters. Will they all let it go? Just forget about it?" Rebecca blew out a breath. "Do you know how humiliating it has been for me to try to keep calm when harassed by reporters? The last one was brutal."

Her father's shoulders slumped. Without making eye contact, he offered, "I know, darling. I'm so sorry."

"Sorry doesn't cut it for me. And how do you plan to explain it to the public?"

He met her glare. "I'll state the facts. We want to stay married."

"What if that's not enough? What if you lose your support?"

"Doesn't matter." His body straightened, and his shoulders squared. "I've given my resignation. I'm retiring. Your mother and I are going to spend time together. Travel, see the world, do all the things we talked about before I let work consume me." He reached for Olivia's hand and softly kissed it.

"Sounds wonderful, but do you think you can forgive and forget? I mean lying to each other. That certainly isn't something I could forgive."

Olivia shrugged. "Sometimes forgiveness is worth it." Her smile seemed genuinely sincere. "People aren't perfect. We all make mistakes. Even if at the time it seems like no one will get hurt, sometimes it backfires. You hurt the people you love the most."

"Rebecca, you're an attorney—"

"Assistant attorney, Dad," she corrected. She heard a soft chuckle from her mother.

"I stand corrected." He grinned. "As an assistant attorney, you know things aren't always black and white. His expression turned serious. "You flip the question over and look at both sides, and then decide what the truth is. And as for yourself, you decide if the truth is worth forgiveness or not."

Olivia added, "Frank and I feel our love is worth fighting to save."

Rebecca found herself saying, "I suppose. I'm not sure I could forgive someone for downright lying."

Her mother took her hand and lightly squeezed it. "Most importantly, Rebecca, can you forgive us?"

While some of her wanted to reject the idea of them getting back together, she also wanted her family to be whole. She wanted everything to be as it had been when she was growing up and living at home. She loved both of her parents with her entire heart. Of course, she could forgive them. Her wish was for them to be happy. If being together again made them happy, she could forgive and try even harder to forget. Still, she wasn't sure she could forgive as quickly if the situation ever happened to her.

"Yes. Of course, I forgive you both. And I'm happy for you."

"Oh, my precious daughter. Thank you." She let out a relieved sigh.

"Thank you, honey." Her father leaned closer and said, "And now we'll tell you our other news."

"There's more?"

Her father beamed with his statement. "We're renewing our vows."

"We'll have a wonderful party," Olivia exclaimed. "We'll make it the event of the year. With your help, of course."

Rebecca laughed softly. Finally, she surrendered and nodded in agreement. As insane as this sounded to her, it was their decision. "Of course, I'll help." She patted her mother's hand. "Let's see. We'll need a location, a menu, and a cake. I better get started making a list."

List. Rebecca grinned. Would her parent's renewal of vows list be as fun to write as the one she made for Mick? Which reminded her. "Mom, I know where we can get the perfect band for your party."

"That's wonderful, darling. I knew you'd be supportive." Her mother leaned over and hugged her.

"Rebecca," her father said quietly. "I haven't asked. Anything new on your latest case?"

"It's going quite well. In fact, during my research, I discovered some undeclared holdings throughout several eastern states. Of course, I can't give you any details, but Mr. Whittaker is building quite a case against the other side."

"Good job. I'll be following your work. And if I can be of any help, remember, ask."

"Thank you, Dad."

"All right, my two loves," her father announced. "I need to get back to work. I have a lot to do before I leave office." With that said, he placed his napkin next to the side of his plate and stood. "Rebecca, this has been delightful." He turned to Olivia. "My darling, I will see you tonight."

Rebecca downed the last of her wine as soon as her father left. "Don't worry, Mom, I'll take care of everything. Make your second honeymoon plans and think about what you'll wear."

Rebecca's steps were light as she headed back to the office. Her mind churned with ideas for her parents' renewal party. Plus, she decided she cared about Mick, and it was time to tell him everything. No more secrets. She wondered why she had put it off for so long, and suddenly her heart felt lighter.

Chapter Eight

Mick helped unload the last of their equipment and instruments from the back of Rafe's truck while trying to ignore the weird stare from his friend. Finally, it got the better of him. "Go ahead, Rafe, ask your questions." With a shake of his head, he added. "Won't do you any good, though."

Rafe let out a bark of laughter. "Hey, none of my business. Just can't help but wonder what's got you so absent-minded."

Mick nodded. "Yeah, I already apologized for forgetting about tonight. But I'm here, aren't I?"

"You're here. Hope you can remember the words to some songs."

"Get a life."

"I got one. And I think you do as well. Got it bad from what I'm seeing."

"F you."

Rafe laughed harder. "Hey, it's not a bad thing. We all fall for someone at some point. I hope it works out great for you."

"Thanks. Have my doubts, though. I haven't told Reb who I am."

"What do you mean?" Looking curious, Rafe asked, "Who you are?"

"I mean, she only knows me as Mick, a guy who plays music occasionally at a biker bar. She doesn't know the real me."

"You mean she doesn't know you're Michael W. Harris, tax attorney. And, if all goes as planned, a soon-to-be partner in the company?"

"Nope."

"She doesn't know when you're not riding your Harley, that you're driving a Beamer. Not to mention the recently purchased vacation home in Hawaii?"

"Nope."

"Holy crap." Rafe lifted an amplifier from the bed of the truck. "That's cool, though. She likes you for you. Not your money."

"She likes the side she's seen." But he knew how much she disliked deceit. She'd made that fact clear to him. Her job was to protect women from men who weren't truthful.

Rafe smirked. "Who wouldn't like a rich dude?"

"Maybe Reb."

"So, tell her. Find out how she feels."

"I'm waiting for the right moment." Mick closed the tailgate to Rafe's truck.

Rafe shrugged. "If my girlfriend surprised me that she was loaded, hell, I'd jump for joy."

"Hey!" Danny shouted from the bar's back doorway. "What's going on out there? We need to get set up."

Mick jerked his attention toward their drummer. "Coming."

"Seriously, it's no big deal," Rafe casually said as he headed across the parking lot. "Don't worry about it. She'll be thrilled. Call her later and tell her."

"Maybe." Mick shook his head as he picked up his guitar case and followed Rafe. He couldn't help but worry. So far, his relationship with Reb was based on lies. Mick wasn't ready for the moment she realized he was just like every other guy she'd ever dated. He wasn't wild and wasn't living a carefree life free of obligations, and she'd see him for what he was a fraud.

# # #

Despite going through what seemed to be the most challenging period of her life, Rebecca felt better than she had in weeks. The almost divorce of her parents had been overwhelming, but now, it was like a bad dream. Even the TV interview seemed like it had happened years ago instead of a couple of days.

She glanced at her watch. She needed to get a move on if she hoped to miss the morning rush hour traffic. Rebecca swallowed the last of her coffee and then ran to the living room to gather her computer and the files she'd worked on last night. She was almost ready to leave the house when her phone rang. Frowning, she removed it from her handbag while wondering who would call her this early.

"Good morning, beautiful," came Mick's cheerful greeting.

Her tummy tingled at the sound of his voice. "Good morning, yourself."

"I was wondering if you had any plans for tonight. I know it's last minute, but I was gifted two tickets to the symphony. Before I give them away, I thought I'd see if you'd enjoy getting dressed and going out on the town."

"I'd love it." Fantastic, she thought. Tonight will be the perfect time to tell him who I am, and then I'll ask him to play music for my parent's renewal party.

"Great. Are you sure it will be exciting enough for you?"

"It will if I don't wear any underwear."

Mick answered after a long pause. "Reb. Wow, Reb."

"Yes, Mick?" The seductive siren voice escaping Rebecca's lips both surprised and delighted her.

"Just wow," he repeated. "You sure know how to catch a guy off guard."

"That was my intention. Now think about that visual all day. Bye." She smiled, completely happy with herself. Playing with Reb's personality might e wrong but was such fun.

Rebecca made it through the rest of her hectic workday, still smiling. Surprisingly, the hours flew by, but they had been chaotic and swamped due to the case they were working on, which caused her to leave the office later than she had hoped. The luxurious bath she'd planned earlier turned into a quick shower.

After a refreshing shower using her favorite vanilla-scented gel and shampoo, she felt renewed. She wasted no time blowing out her hair and sweeping it up with a large clip. A minimum of liquid makeup, a dab of blush followed by mascara, pink lipstick, and a spray of her favorite perfume, with an extra spritz between her breasts, and she was ready. Prepared for whatever the evening brought her way.

Rummaging through her closet, she finally settled on a low-cut, wrap-around, black cocktail dress. Happy with how the outfit accentuated her every curve, she added a diamond drop pendent, her favorite diamond bracelet, and a pair of strappy high heels. Not bad, she thought as she gazed into her full-length mirror.

The doorbell rang, and she glanced at the clock on her nightstand—Mick, punctual as usual.

"Just a second," she yelled.

She ran to the door, pulled it open, and stood, staring into Mick's dark blue eyes.

"Come on in." She stepped aside, breathing in his masculine scent as he walked past her and into the room.

"You look amazing." He kissed her tenderly on the cheek.

"You look pretty good, yourself." She let her gaze travel from his face down his body, admiring how his dress jeans and the crisp, white shirt perfectly fit him. With his looks and talent, it was no wonder women packed Mo's bar on ladies' night.

Pulling her closer, he skimmed his hands over her hips and whispered near her ear, "I don't feel any panty lines."

She giggled. "No?" Thank goodness for thong underwear. She wasn't about to reveal her secret yet. Let him assume for a while that she'd fulfilled her earlier statement and wore nothing under her dress.

As they walked toward the door, Rebecca felt his hand touch her back. A warm sensation shot tingles through her body. Even through her dress, his fingers left heat trails on her skin.

"Oh, I forgot to ask. Would you like me to drive?"

"Not tonight." He winked. "Got us covered."

After she locked the front door of her condo, he walked her toward the driveway. The glow of a beautiful Arizona sunset lit the sky, outlining a shiny black BMW.

"Nice car. How did you get this?"

"Don't worry, Reb," he said as he opened the passenger door. "I wanted to make you feel special. You deserve it."

"You're full of surprises, Mick." Rebecca smiled as she slid inside the car.

He returned her smile and then stood silently for a long moment. Rebecca thought he was about to say something, but instead, he closed the passenger door and walked around to the driver's side.

Putting the car into reverse, he slowly backed out of the driveway. Within minutes they were driving through the traffic-filled street heading east toward downtown Scottsdale.

Rebecca smiled happily to herself. Her need to confess her identity was the only thing holding back complete joy. And tonight, she would. Once they were back home after the concert. Then, she'd invite him to sing at her parents' party. She could visualize the surprise on his face when she told him how much they would pay for his performance. She'd bet it was more than he made at Mo's for one night.

Rebecca usually hated heavy traffic, but tonight she barely noticed. She was having such a good time, laughing at Mick's silly jokes. Both singing along with the radio, she a little off key, Mick not making fun of her lack of musical talent. He made her feel like an actual princess.

They stopped at a red light, and Mick turned the music down. "Thank you for coming with me tonight."

"Thank you for inviting me. It's been a long time since I've been on an actual date. This is nice."

"You don't date much? I'm surprised. A beautiful woman like yourself, I'd think you'd have your pick of guys."

"No. Most of the guys I've dated only cared about themselves. Their idea of a conversation was telling me how much money they'd made in the stock market or how many closings they'd had over the week.

"No nice guys in your little black book?"

"No little black book, period."

"Why not?"

Oh, she could answer that quickly enough. She almost blurted because I'm a senator's daughter, a daughter of someone they could use to further their career. She leaned her head back against the headrest. Thank goodness she wouldn't have to watch her words much longer. After tonight, Mick would know the truth, but for now, she still had to be careful.

Rebecca licked her lips. "Busy. Finishing college. Starting a career. No time to date."

"I get it. I can see how that could easily happen."

She hadn't lied. Passing law school and starting her career had kept her busy.

Rebecca divided any free time between the women's shelter and helping her mother with charity fundraising. She had actual excuses to blow off men asking her for a date.

She had her girlfriends. Trisha, Scarlett, and Rayna. After college, they'd introduced her to Arizona's nightlife. With them, Rebecca found a new world of fun and adventure, and she liked it. She could be wild and free; no one knew she was a politician's daughter. She could pretend to be anyone she wanted.

That is until she met Mick. Somehow, she hated deceiving him. But when she told him the truth, would he see her as a stuck-up, little rich girl getting her kicks with a poor musician? Would he be uncomfortable meeting her parents? She sighed heavily.

"Let's talk about you." She needed to change the subject. Clearing her throat, she asked. "When did you decide you wanted to become a musician?"

"Far back as I can remember. I was thirteen when I got my first guitar." He paused. "Then my mom got sick, and I poured all my grief into the music."

"Oh, Mick, I'm so sorry."

"Thanks. Yeah, those were rough years. Pretty hard on my dad, and after she passed, he went into a deep depression." With a shrug, he added, "I had my music to help me."

Rebecca didn't have any words for the first time in her life.

Chapter Nine

Rebecca took it all in, mesmerized by the entire symphony experience. As she settled into her seat, she let her mind wander back to her tenth birthday. Her parents had taken her to her first concert, and that evening she fell in love with how music could make you feel.

Tonight, she felt almost giddy. Sitting next to Mick, surrounded by people nicely dressed, all happily smiling, waiting to be swept away by a performance of magical musical talent.

The house lighting dimmed, and Mick reached for her hand. Tingles spread through her body as his fingers squeezed lightly. She leaned toward him, drawn by his warmth, his presence beside her.

"Tonight is wonderful," she whispered.

Mick lowered his lips close to her ear. "And it's not over yet."

His breath sent tingles shooting down her neck and straight to her heart. She offered him a soft laugh. She knew he wasn't only talking about the musical performance. The thought of him making love to her, caressing her body with his skilled fingers, strumming her skin as if she were his beloved guitar, heated her to her core. No one had ever made her feel like Mick.

Smiling, she let herself relax into the plush seat, tilting her head upward to appreciate the rhythm of the woodwinds. Her eyes drifted shut as violins began to fill the space around her and her heart picked up speed as the soaring music pulsed harder.

Mick's hand tightened around hers before bringing it to his mouth. She let out a gentle breath as his lips brushed slowly across each of her knuckles. Her nipples pressed firmly against the fabric of her dress.

Without hesitation, she lowered their hands to Mick's lap and let the back of hers lightly brush across the zipper of his pants. Even though she figured no one was paying any attention to them in the darkened theatre, the public act was thrilling. Never had she done anything so bold. Mercy, it was fun being Reb.

Mick leaned into Reb and whispered, "When I get you alone, you're going to get—"

"Shh," she cut him off. Then freeing her hand from his, she replied, "Enjoy the music."

He chuckled, then slid his hand under the hem of her dress to touch her thigh. As her skin heated under his caress, he muttered. "I'm thinking about your no underwear idea."

"You keep thinking about that."

"Damn, girl, I'm not sure I can make it through the program."

#

"I'm glad you had a good time tonight, Reb. I wasn't sure how you'd feel about going to a symphony."

"Are you kidding? She gushed, "It was wonderful."

"I'm happy you feel that way." Mick rested his hand on Reb's shoulder as they walked out of the lobby and headed toward the parking garage.

"Mick, this has been one of the best nights of my life."

"Remember what I told you earlier. This night's not over, so maybe before it is, I can make it your best night ever." He pulled her closer.

"Maybe you can," she answered, giggling.

Mick concentrated on Reb, completely caught up in the moment. They walked in step with each other until they reached their car. Mick hit the unlock button on the fob, still holding Reb tight. "Hungry?"

"Actually, I am."

"What's your preference?"

"How about Mexican?"

"A taco or two sounds good."

"Hey, there, Michael!" A man's voice called from nearby.

Hearing his name, Mick automatically glanced toward the sound, then cringed.

A tall man in his forties with sandy, short, cropped hair stood a mere two vehicles away, waving toward them.

Busted. Big time. James Hill. The man was one of his latest clients. Mick forced a smile and waved back. As sweat broke across his forehead, he silently willed the man to turn and leave. No such luck.

Mr. Hill took a step closer. "Great to see you—"

"Jim, the babysitter called. Julie won't go to bed." The blonde woman standing next to Mr. Hill's SUV interrupted.

He answered, "All right." He looked back toward Mick and shrugged. "Kid problems. I'll call you soon. Have a nice night."

Mick nodded. "Thank you. Looking forward to your call."

Mick took a deep breath and opened the passenger door.

Reb turned her gaze to him. "Who was that?"

He stood with one hand folded over the top of the door while looking off to the side. He knew he would lie and couldn't meet Reb's eyes. He shrugged. "I don't know. Someone from Mo's, I guess."

After a perplexed pause, Reb murmured, "Oh." She slid inside the car and buckled her seat belt. "Didn't he call you Michael?"

"Did he?"

Before he closed the door, he leaned in, kissed her on the cheek, then walked to the driver's side. The lying had to stop. He couldn't do it anymore. Tonight, she would know everything there was to know about him. Lord help him, she'd understand.

He felt her eyes watch him get in, start the engine, and back out of the parking spot.

"Are you okay?" Reb asked when he pulled from the garage onto the street.

He nodded. "I'm fine." Forcing a laugh, he added, "Just looking forward to a taco."

What sounded good to him at the moment was a double shot of tequila.

Chapter Ten

The twenty-minute drive from downtown Scottsdale to the Mexican restaurant went quickly. Rebecca and Mick chatted about their evening, her natural personality spilling out as she recalled the beautiful music they'd enjoyed at the symphony. From there, the conversation moved on to sharing the genres they listened to at home alone. Then they listed all the live concerts they had attended, wondering if they had been to any simultaneously.

Mostly Rebecca was curious to learn what inspired Mick when he wrote love songs. She laughed when he told her it was his childhood dog. Even though she knew that wasn't the truth, the visual of him serenading a floppy-eared pup endeared her to him more.

The night was perfect except for the tiny white lie hanging over Rebecca's head. She wished she could say the words in her heart. Tell him how she'd grown up under the strict rules set in place by her parents—especially her father, who was a well-known politician. She was an assistant attorney who worked in a prestigious law firm, not a newly hired research intern like she'd led him to believe.

Of course, he'd find out the truth soon enough. Tonight, she vowed, and that is if she kept her nerve up. She leaned back in the car's seat and worried her bottom lip as they traveled the last mile in silence.

Rebecca expected the restaurant to be crowded, and it didn't fall short of her expectations. Mick circled the parking lot twice before a spot opened.

"Hope we can get in without a reservation," he told her as he whipped the BMW into the vacant space.

She nodded in agreement.

Within minutes they were walking through the front entrance.

"Any chance we can get a table?" Mick asked the young hostess.

"No problem. There's a private party in the back room, which is why we look so busy. Follow me."

Piped-in Mariachi music accompanied them to a colorful, inlaid tiled table near the stage. On the way, the hostess informed them that the regular band was performing for the party, but they had a lesser-known group scheduled to play soon.

"Thanks," Mick said as he pulled out a chair for Rebecca.

The hostess placed menus on the table as they settled into their seats. "Your server will be here shortly. Enjoy."

Rebecca glanced up from her menu and caught Mick staring at her. He looked as if he wanted to say something, but the waitress interrupted before she could ask what was on his mind.

They both ordered margaritas on the rocks with salted rims. Then after considerable negotiation, they decided to share a chicken and shrimp fajita platter along with some shredded beef tacos. Mick asked for extra guacamole and sour cream for them both.

Rebecca inhaled deeply as a heaping bowl of warm tortilla chips was placed in front of them, accompanied by two different types of salsas. Her mouth began to water as the spicy aroma surrounded them.

Their drinks arrived. Happily, Rebecca raised her margarita glass. "To a great dinner."

"I'll drink to that." Their glasses clinked lightly.

Mick immediately took a long swallow from his drink.

Rebecca brought her cocktail to her lips and tasted the salt, the zesty lime juice, and the robust and flavorful tequila. Then she picked up a chip from the bowl and scooped a generous amount of salsa.

"Oh, my, this is delicious, Mick," she said after she savored her first bite loaded with the dip. She pushed the bowl toward him. "Have one."

"I love to watch you eat."

She let out a soft laugh. "You say that to all the girls?"

"Only you, darling."

She blushed and glanced away just in time to see their waitress heading toward them carrying their entrees.

Dinner didn't disappoint. The chef grilled the meat and vegetables perfectly with precisely enough char and chili seasonings.

"By the way, I've been meaning to ask you something," Rebecca said while spearing a shrimp from the sizzling platter.

"About what?"

"Would you consider singing at my parent's renewal of vows celebration?"

He looked startled for a moment as if processing what she'd said. "Renewal of vows?"

"Mom and Dad had some problems that they worked out. They're throwing a party."

He straightened in his chair. "Reb, I'm not sure I should do that."

"Are you kidding? You're perfect." Tilting her head slightly, she gave him a puppy dog look. "Oh, please, Mick, come on." She raised her eyebrows. "And here's the big bonus, the payment for the evening will be great."

Mick's fork stopped halfway to his mouth. He lowered it and leaned forward. "Reb, there is no way I'm taking money from you."

"Not from me. From my parents."

"Same thing."

"Well, actually, it's not."

"To me, it is." He set his fork down and pushed back his plate. "The answer is no."

"No to the money or no to singing at their party?" Wow. His reaction was certainly wasn't the one she'd expected. Why wasn't he excited?

He puffed a slow breath, picked up his drink, and drained the glass.

"All right. All right," Rebecca said after a moment. "I just thought it would be a good opportunity for you. Plus, it'll be a fun evening."

"Let me think about it. But let's get one thing straight. No money, Understand."

"Fine. I got it. No money. But you'll do it, right?" Uneasiness swept across her shoulders.

A moment of silence passed between them.

"Oh, hell, sure. I'll do it." He gazed at her with a cautious expression. "But how do you know your parents will like me?"

"Mick, there's no question about that, and it's simple. Because I like you."

He didn't answer. He only stared, making her feel like he was trying to read her mind. Rebecca nibbled her lower lip while trying to figure out what he could be thinking. He looked worried. Perhaps he believed he wouldn't get her parents' approval? Of course, that was silly. They'd see Mick the same way she did. As a warm, caring, sincere man with a lot of talent. She'd make that clear.

Of course, there was still the small matter she needed to get out in the open. She had to let Mick know who her parents were and who she was. She smiled nervously. She reminded herself that everything would be out in the open later tonight. And, of course, he'd understand. It would be a joke they'd laugh about in the future.

Shaking off her emotions, she picked up her glass and brought it to her lips.

"Is there something else?"

She blinked. "What?"

"You look preoccupied."

Good a time as ever, she thought. "I have something I'd like to tell you."

"Sounds serious. Go ahead. You have my complete attention." A smile curved his lips. "Can't be worse than the last thing you sprang on me."

Oh, yes, maybe it is, she thought. She sucked in a steadying breath and slowly released it. Then cleared her throat and willed her Reb personality to bubble up and help her sound strong. Silly to be nervous. For crying out loud, she spoke before crowds with no problem. Decision made. Steeling herself by drinking the last swallow of her margarita, she met his questioning gaze. "Mick, I'm actually—"

"Hey! Fancy seeing you two here."

Startled, Rebecca looked up to see Scarlett standing next to their table. Her friend was stunning, wearing a low-cut black T-shirt and long silver earrings. Her wavy, reddish hair gleamed in the restaurant's lighting as the illumination caught each curl.

"What a surprise." Reb motioned toward the empty chair Mick had scooted out from the table. "Join us."

"We'd love to." Scarlett slid into the chair across from Rebecca while motioning to the tall man wearing a black cowboy hat standing behind her also to sit. "You remember David, right? From the place out in Cave Creek."

"Um, sure. Hi." Rebecca remembered that night well. The dancing had been fun, but she'd gone to breakfast with someone she had no desire to see again. Hopefully, Scarlett wouldn't bring that part up. "Mick. My friend Scarlett."

Mick nodded. "Nice to see you again."

Scarlett focused on Mick while pointing toward the guy at her side. "This is David."

"Pleasure to meet you. Yes, please join us." Mick gestured toward the other empty chair.

"Mick plays with a band at a bar called Mo's." Scarlett gushed enthusiastically before her date could speak. Then she turned toward David, "you've heard of Mo's, right?"

He eased into the chair next to Scarlett and removed his cowboy hat, revealing a head of unruly blond locks. While running tanned fingers through his hair, he leaned forward and smiled. "I think so. Nice to meet you."

Mick flashed a smile, then raised a hand to their waitress, motioning for her to come to the table. "What are you two drinking?"

"Those margaritas look great," Scarlett stated, pointing toward the drinks on the table.

"They're delicious," Rebecca agreed as she glanced at her almost empty glass.

"Sound good to you?" Mick asked David. When Scarlett's date nodded, he told the waitress, "Margaritas all around."

As the four of them sat making small talk and laughing, Rebecca couldn't help worrying. Thank goodness, Scarlett hadn't said anything incriminating like going to bars using an alias looking for their Mr. Right—so far.

Another reminder to Rebecca of how she needed to get the truth out in the open soon. This stupid white lie was going to give her an ulcer.

Chapter Eleven

The band at the restaurant had taken the stage and started to play a familiar, upbeat song. One Mick sang quite often at Mo's. Scarlett and David were headed out on the dance floor, leaving him alone with Reb. He had to admit he enjoyed the company of her friends, but in truth, he was glad to have her all to himself for a few minutes.

The desire to get everything out in the open rumbled through him. It had to be done, for better or worse. Tonight, he figured, was the time. Once he had Reb comfortably back at her house, they'd have an honest talk. Starting with his confession that music was only a part-time venture for him. He wasn't a bad boy musician at heart and singing with the band at Mo's was simply a hobby he enjoyed.

Mick's mind concentrated on the second thing he'd admit. He'd tell her that his profession was as a tax attorney, and in a few weeks, if all went well, he'd be made a partner with the firm. If she questioned his career choice, he'd tell her the truth. Tax law came easy for him. He had a strong understanding of math rules. Explaining complicated tax laws to clients so they could make sound decisions gave him pleasure and made him feel proud. What didn't make him proud was that he'd lied to Reb in the first place.

Mick glanced toward Reb and noticed her staring at him. He smiled.

She smiled, too, then took a sip of her margarita.

He loved how she looked tonight, with her hair pulled up in a clip exposing her lovely neck. He watched as she brought the margarita to her pink, luscious lips and sipped through the straw. He wanted to kiss her and taste the tequila on her tongue. He took a deep breath to suppress the urge.

Why had he led her to believe he was happy to play music part-time in a biker bar? He knew the answer. She had clarified that she wanted a stimulating, uncomplicated, not dull lifestyle. And he would do anything to show her that's how he lived his life.

Oh, sure, playing the role of a carefree musician was fun. And he had to admit using his imagination to create unusual places for wild sex was incredible. But the craziness could only go on for so long. The truth would come out. It had almost happened tonight in the parking garage when they ran into one of his clients. And if he was being honest with himself, it was becoming exhausting. His hands slid beneath the table and rubbed the fabric covering his knees. Just thinking about having this conversation made his palms sweat.

He straightened in his seat and placed his hands on the table. Another thing he needed to clear up was why he'd been hesitant about singing at her parents' party. He couldn't meet them under a pretense. And he definitely wouldn't take money from them. After all, he was falling in love with their daughter. Everything had to be entirely out in the open when he met them.

Even if it would be hard for him to admit his deception, Reb deserved to know the truth. Afterward, when she understood and had forgiven him, he would make love to her as himself with no more lies between them. No more of him trying to give her a false impression. A grin tickled his lips. Oh, yeah, tonight was going to work out just fine. He picked up his drink and took a long swallow.

The song ended, and another one started. Scarlett and David stayed out on the floor.

"Looks like those two are having fun." Reb pointed toward the dance floor.

"Yeah," he agreed. "They seem to be enjoying themselves."

"Are you having a good time?" she asked. "I hope it was okay to invite them to join us."

"Sure." Mick glanced toward the dancers again. "I like Scarlett, and David seems like a nice enough guy. He let his gaze return to hers. "You were about to tell me something before they sat down."

Her eyes darted downward momentarily, then glanced at him. "It can wait."

"Okay. If you're sure?"

"I'm sure."

"You know, you can tell me anything." Hopefully, this would go both ways, he thought.

She nodded.

Deciding not to press her, he pushed back his chair and stood. "Come dance with me."

Her eyes lit. "I'd love to."

She took his hand, and he walked her to the dance floor. In his arms, desire washed over him as he deeply breathed in her perfume. She rested her cheek against him and slid her fingers through the hair at the nape of his neck. Mick's heart rate increased, and it felt perfect holding her. He pulled her closer and started humming along with the music, oblivious to the other couples dancing nearby.

When the song ended, hand in hand, they headed back toward their table. Halfway across the floor, someone from the stage yelled. "Hey, Harris. Is that you?"

They both turned to see one of the guys in the band standing near the edge of the stage.

Mick waved.

"Do you know the band?" Reb asked.

"I know that guy. We used to mess around on guitars back in the day."

"Wow. There's so much I don't know about you."

"About that. We need to talk later. I have—"

"Hey, everybody." The guy with the microphone hollered. "Look who we have in the house. Mick Harris. Let's get him up here for a song."

The audience applauded, and someone gave a loud whistle.

Mick glanced around.

"Go on, Mick, please," Reb urged.

Mick shrugged. "You sure you don't mind?"

"Are you serious? I love hearing you sing. Go on. Serenade me with a love song."

He kissed her cheek and squeezed her hand. "Stay where I can see you."

The dance floor crowd parted, and he moved toward the stage. He greeted his friend, then after a few words were exchanged between them he signaled the band as he stepped to the microphone.

"You got it, Mick," the drummer answered, and he immediately gave the guys a four-beat cue on the snare's rim.

He made eye contact with Reb, who stood off the side of the dance floor. She made a heart sign with her fingers. Scarlett and David had joined her, grinning and clapping loudly at his announcement.

Mick started singing the words he knew so well.

"Tonight. Who knew...I'd find you here tonight?"

He winked, and she smiled.

"Waiting for so long, for someone...for you."

Chapter Twelve

"You made me happy tonight," Rebecca told Mick as they walked into her house. "I loved it when you sang our song. I don't think I've ever felt so special." She giggled. "Not to mention, I think you made every woman in the restaurant envious of me."

"Every woman in the restaurant was envious because you're so beautiful."

"You think I'm beautiful?" Reb asked thoughtfully.

"Reb, you are the most beautiful woman I've ever laid my eyes on." Mick pulled her closer. "Beautiful inside and out."

She opened her mouth to speak, but the words wouldn't come. She couldn't ruin the moment, and there'd be time to talk in the morning. Letting out a sigh, she let him hold her tightly, her cheek pressed against his chest. She inhaled his masculine scent as her eyes drifted closed and whispered more to herself than to him, "I hope you always feel this way."

Visions of him leaving when he learned the truth about her played vividly in her mind. Of course, that was silly for her to think that way. Why would finding out she was successful, and her father was a well-known politician be a problem? If anything, Mick would be proud. After all, it had taken a lot of work to get where she was in her career. Rebecca let out a sigh, then inwardly scolded herself for letting her thoughts wander toward the negative. Be like Reb, a wild, kick-ass woman. Think positive like the strong woman you've become. Tell the truth and expect positive results.

"Don't you know how crazy I am about you?" his hands began caressing her shoulders.

Willing herself back to the present, she whispered, "I'm crazy about you, too." Her arms wrapped around his neck, "Kiss me, Mick."

He obeyed, dipping to catch her mouth, parting his lips, allowing her to ravage his mouth with her tongue. At that moment, Rebecca believed she was beautiful. Mick made her feel irresistible, and he made her feel powerful. He made her feel like she was a rebel, which felt fantastic.

There was no way she'd let this man get away from her. No matter how often she told herself she didn't want a Mr. Right, Mick had changed all that. She loved him. Breaking their kiss, she reached up, ran her fingers along his cheek, and then offered a smile. "Take me to bed."

Again, without hesitation, he did as she asked.

At the entrance of her bedroom, they were met with the soft glow from the butterfly-shaped night light near the far wall. It seemed as if several lit candles illuminated the space making for a romantic ambiance.

Mick stepped closer and pulled her into his arms again. He gently removed the clip from her hair, letting the thick curls fall about her shoulders. Then he moved his hand lower down her back, trailing his fingers along her spine.

She couldn't keep the hunger for him from escaping. "I want you inside me."

"I want that, too." His voice was low and deep near her ear. She shivered as his breath brushed her skin.

Mick tugged the tie of her wraparound dress, allowing it to fall open. He pushed the material off her shoulders and let it slide to pool around her ankles, lightly caressing her skin as it became uncovered.

"What's this," he asked as his fingers skimmed the edge of her panties. "I thought there was a no underwear deal."

"Well, in case you haven't noticed, I'm not wearing a bra."

He chuckled. "Oh, I noticed." He leaned in and kissed the top curve of her breast. Then he slid his tongue lower to slowly lick across her hardened nipple.

When his mouth closed around the stiff peak, and he sucked deep, she whimpered, "Oh, Mick...."

He scooped her up, carried her over to the bed, and sank onto the mattress, pulling her down with him. She straddled his lap and gripped his shoulders as he kissed her again. Pushing him back, she worked his pants down so he could get rid of them along with his shoes. Next, she removed his shirt, letting her fingers run across his bare chest.

"Will you do something else for me?"

He didn't hesitate. "Anything you want."

"Stay with me tonight. I want to tell you something. We have things to get out in the open."

"I know."

She gazed at him with a cautious expression. "You do?"

Reaching up to cup her face in his hand, he stared into her questioning eyes. "Yes. I know we need to talk. I have things I need to say. And we should right now, but at this moment, all I can think about is how much I want you."

He rolled her onto her back. Abandoning the promise she'd made to herself to tell him the truth tonight, she closed her eyes and welcomed his body as it covered hers.

"Coffee's ready," Mick called toward the bedroom.

He watched her walk into the kitchen, letting his gaze travel from her neatly brushed hair to her high-heeled shoes. As he handed her a steaming mug of his brew, his fingers gently brushed hers, and his heart tightened. How long should he wait before starting the truth-telling conversation? Before breakfast or after they'd finished eating. "Good morning."

"Good morning." She took a sip of the coffee. Smiled and gave a nod of appreciation.

"I scrambled some eggs." He pointed to the skillet on the stove.

"I had no idea you cooked. Thank you." She picked up a plate and scooped some of the eggs onto it.

"You're welcome," he replied.

They sat at the breakfast nook, drinking coffee and eating the eggs in silence. Her perfume drifted across the table. The smell of it made shivers dance across his shoulders. Sitting with her like this was a perfect start to the day. He smiled, completely caught in the moment.

"So, what did you want to talk about this morning?" Reb asked, breaking the silence between them.

"We need to talk about us," he said.

"Yeah, I know," She answered, avoiding his eyes. "Mick, I have something I need to tell you. I didn't want to ruin last night."

Her words surprised him. He was the one who needed to explain his reasons for not telling her the truth. Whatever she had to say couldn't be as bad as what he had to tell her. Or maybe it was worse. "Okay…is it going to be bad news?"

"Not at all. But I'm not sure how you'll feel about it."

Mick reached over to place his hand on top of hers. His heartbeat raced. Was she going to tell him that they should take things slower? Was she planning to dump him? No, that couldn't be correct. She'd told him how much she cared for him. "It's all right, Reb. I'm not pressing our relationship if that's how you feel. But before you break my heart, there's something I need to tell you as well."

"Oh, no, Mick. You've got the wrong idea. The last thing I want is for our relationship to end. That's why I want to be honest with you."

Mick breathed a sigh of relief. At least she wasn't breaking up with him. Not yet anyway. "That's what I want for us as well, Reb. Complete honesty."

They both startled at the sound of her cell phone.

"I'm sorry, I should check that. It might be the office." She pointed to her phone sitting on the counter near the toaster.

"Of course." Mick smiled as he watched her scoot from her chair and rushed toward the ringing phone. He picked up his mug and swallowed the now lukewarm coffee. Deciding this would be an excellent time to get a refill, he stood, then stopped as he noticed the look of panic on Reb's face.

"Oh, no, Scarlett. What happened?" Rebecca yelled into the phone.

Mick quickly moved to her side and placed his hand on her shoulder.

"Of course. I'll meet you there." She let out a sigh and then turned to meet his questioning eyes. "I need to go to the hospital. My friend's been in an accident."

"Scarlett?"

"It's Rayna. A car accident, but Scarlett didn't have the details."

"I'll take you."

"No," she protested. "Thank you. I'll be okay. I need to leave for the office after I check on Rayna."

"Okay," he agreed, then stepped closer to give her a comforting hug.

"Tonight, we'll talk. I promise." Reb broke their embrace, grabbed her purse and car keys then headed toward the door. "I'll call you with an update. Stay and finish your coffee. Bye."

Mick heard the garage door open, then, minutes later, close. He drew a shuddering breath, turned, and started placing their dishes in the dishwasher. "Tonight," he muttered. Then he added quietly, "this is going to be a long day."

Chapter Thirteen

"Rayna," Rebecca whispered, entering the hospital room. "Are you okay?" Her heart ached for Rayna, who looked pale and helpless lying on the narrow bed hooked up to an IV drip. In the corner, a heart monitor signaled steadily.

"I'll be fine." Rayna shifted slightly, removed the blanket draped across her, and pointed to her swollen and purple-blotched ankle. "I feel so stupid, but I didn't see the car coming in time to react."

"Oh, goodness. Is your ankle broken?"

"Nurse thinks it might be." Rayna winced as she pulled the blanket back over herself. "I'm getting it x-rayed."

Rebecca patted Rayna's hand lovingly, then smiled in greeting toward Scarlett, sitting next to the hospital bed, her perfectly arched brows knitted together in worry.

"Hopefully, my car didn't suffer too much damage," Rayna muttered.

"Don't worry about your car. That's why you have insurance, you're the one we care about." Rebecca stepped closer and smoothed a wisp of pink hair off Rayna's face.

Scarlett set the magazine she'd been flipping through down, stood, and carefully adjusted the pillow behind her friend's head. "You also have a concussion."

"The EMT said I possibly have a slight concussion." Rayna grimaced and leaned back against the pillow.

Rebecca frowned at the word concussion.

The door opened, and Trisha entered the room carrying a large bouquet of fresh flowers. "Hi. I got here as quickly as possible."

"Thank you. The flowers are beautiful." Rayna closed her eyes. "You, girls, are so good to me."

"They gave her some pain meds," Scarlett commented. "She's a bit groggy,"

A woman dressed in scrubs entered, and in her hand was a clipboard. She made her way to Rayna's bedside and smiled. "Just checking your vitals, honey." She glanced at the monitor screen, then jotted a note on her clipboard. "How are you doing?"

"I'm not sure," Rayna replied.

The nurse nodded.

Someone tapped lightly on the door, and they all turned to see a young man enter. Serious dark eyes seemed to access the room before returning to the paperwork in his hand. He glanced up, clearing his throat, "Well, Miss Rayna, it seems you've had a rough morning."

"I've had better." Rayna struggled to sit up straighter on the bed.

"Let's see what we have here." He lifted the blanket off her foot and touched her ankle.

She flinched. "Ouch."

"Sorry." He then introduced himself with an easy grin. "I'm Doctor Cooper." He glanced over her chart again and then read aloud, "No medical history of allergy, asthma, cardiac disease, drug abuse, alcohol, or smoking?"

"None," Rayna answered.

He looked up and smiled again.

Doctor Cooper's smile was friendly, and he had the type of presence that radiates proficiency. At that moment, Rebecca believed her friend was with a medical professional who seriously cared about his patients. She nodded the doctor's approval toward Rayna, who was staring at him with a dreamy expression on her face. Rebecca smiled, wondering if the look in her eyes was because he was so incredibly handsome or because her meds were kicking in.

The door opened, and another person dressed in scrubs entered, pushing a wheelchair.

"I'm sending you for x-rays, and then I'll be back to talk about what we find." Doctor Cooper turned to Rebecca, Scarlett, and Trisha, "You ladies may as well go have some coffee or breakfast. She'll be a while."

Rebecca nodded. "That's a good idea. I could certainly use more coffee." She glanced toward Rayna, who was being helped into the wheelchair. "We'll be back to check on you."

Rayna waved as she was wheeled from the room, followed by the nurse and Doctor Cooper.

Trisha placed the flowers she'd been holding on the tray near the side of the bed. "Do you think she'll be here overnight?"

"Maybe," Scarlett told them. "I'll ask the nurse when she comes back."

"Rayna can't go home by herself," Trisha stated. "Unless her mom or a family member comes to town to stay with her, we'll need to make arrangements."

"She can stay in my guestroom," Rebecca offered. "At least someone would be there at night with her."

"You're too busy with your workload and the renewal party." Trisha continued, "She'll come to stay with me. I can easily work from home."

"And I have vacation days I can take if she needs to get to a doctor's appointment or whatever," Scarlett said.

"Speaking of doctors," Trisha added, changing the subject. "Rayna's is sure hot."

"I agree. Most likely married." Scarlett shrugged. "The good-looking ones always are."

"If I know our Rayna, she'll find out." Rebecca laughed. "Let's go. I'm ready to sit down."

They reached the hospital cafeteria and ordered their coffee. Scarlett selected a sweet roll, a cup of fruit, and her drink. "I haven't had breakfast," she admitted. "You both know how hungry I get when stressed."

"We do," Trisha answered, then laughed.

"I'm good with only coffee," Rebecca said. The image of Mick standing in her kitchen and the tasty eggs he'd fixed flashed in her mind. The memory made her smile.

"I think I'll have one of the rolls myself," Trisha told them. "They look good."

They paid for their items and selected a table near a window. Once seated, Trisha asked Rebecca. "How's your love life going, Rebecca? Still seeing the musician?"

"I am. It's going great." Rebecca took a sip from her Styrofoam cup, then whispered, "Hopefully. it continues."

"Why wouldn't it?" Scarlett asked as she poured cream into her cup. "He sure seemed crazy about you last night. Oh, Trisha, you should have seen them together. They were adorable."

Rebecca smiled. "We did have a nice time. And I intend to tell him the truth about me tonight."

Trisha frowned. "What truth?"

"Yes, what are you talking about?" Scarlett questioned.

"I never told him who I am."

Trisha's eyes widened. "You mean you never told him your name?"

"Oh, I told him my name, but I didn't tell him I'm an attorney or that my dad is a senator."

"For heaven's sake, why not?" Scarlett's voice raised a notch.

Rebecca's friends seemed confused. She caught the look that passed between them.

Could she explain her reasons to them so it would make sense? Rebecca took a deep breath and then blew it out. "I guess I was afraid I would intimidate him. You know, him being a struggling musician. He only plays part-time in a biker bar. He can't make much money." She shrugged. "I don't want to embarrass him."

"That makes absolutely no sense." Trisha tore open a pink sugar packet and emptied it into her coffee.

"No kidding." Scarlett grinned. "He might think you could help his career."

"Another reason." She met their questioning stares. "I want him to like me for being me. Not someone who can help him advance his career, although I would. He's talented. In fact, I asked him to sing at the renewal party. Who knows, he might get booked for more events."

"That offer must have excited him," Trisha asked.

"Actually, no, it didn't. Mick turned me down at first."

"Did he say why?" Trisha questioned.

"Not really." Rebecca's eyebrows pinched together in thought. "I was definitely surprised by his reaction."

"You know, I've always felt something about Mick," Trisha stated. "I think there's more to him than he tells you."

"More to him?" Rebecca questioned, "Like what?"

"I have no idea. I just get a feeling. I can't put my finger on it. Might be good, or maybe bad." Trisha lifted the hair off her neck and added, "I mentioned this to you once, if you remember."

Scarlett leaned forward. "Trisha always has good instincts about reading people."

"I know." Rebecca stared at her coffee cup.

"Have you Googled him?" Trisha asked.

Rebecca confessed. "No."

"You're kidding." Trisha turned her palms up. "That's the first thing I'd have done."

Folding her arms over the cafeteria table, Rebecca leaned forward. "I've been busy."

Scarlett shook her head. "No excuse." Her eyes brightened. "Let's do it now." She picked up her leather tote and began rummaging through it, searching for her phone.

"No. Don't," Rebecca snapped.

Both her friends met her glare. Rebecca shrugged. "Sorry. I don't know. Maybe I'm afraid of what we'll find."

"Okay. If it's bad, we won't tell you," Trisha assured her. "How's that sound?"

"Worse."

"Look, if you don't want us to do a background check on him, we won't," Scarlett promised.

"Right." Rebecca laughed. "I know you both will once I leave the room." What bothered her about checking Mick on the internet? Honestly, what could they possibly discover? "Oh, go ahead. See what you find."

"What's his last name?" Scarlett asked.

"Harris."

Scarlett's fingers went to work on her phone. After a few seconds of scrolling, she announced, "Here he is. Mick Harris musician. Humm, he's got lots of five-star reviews."

Rebecca smiled as she pushed a strand of hair behind her ear. "That doesn't surprise me."

Scarlett continued thumbing through pictures while making little sounds of approval.

Rebecca breathed a sigh of relief. He's exactly who he said he was, she thought.

"Oh, my God!" Scarlett screeched as she shoved her phone toward Trisha, "Look."

"Wow," Trisha whispered. Her gaze turned toward Rebecca's questioning stare.

Rebecca's heart rate jumped a beat. "What?" She asked anxiously, her eyebrows knitting.

"Just look!" Scarlett thrust her phone toward Rebecca, waving it in front of her.

"Hold still. I can't make out anything with you shaking it at me." She grabbed the phone from her friend and concentrated on what had surprised them so much. "Oh..." Rebecca murmured. Her throat tightened. Suddenly the room grew still as her pulse pounded in her temples. For a brief second, she thought she might faint.

She blinked, trying to focus on the picture staring back at her from the screen. A handsome man in a dark grey suit, blue shirt, the color matching his eyes, and a killer smile leaned against a black BMW. Michael W. Harris, soon to be a partner with Marks, Taylor & Cohn. The article went on to describe his accomplishments. Rebecca couldn't read anymore, and her brain couldn't focus. She handed the phone back to Scarlett, then turned to the window and stared blankly outside.

Mick? This couldn't be correct, could it? Different scenarios zoomed through her mind. He must be posing in front of a friend's car. Wait, it says partner. He's a tax attorney? Good Lord, he's playing games with me!

Chapter Fourteen

It was late afternoon when Mick walked into Mo's bar. The day had been long and hectic at the office. He'd met with five separate clients, all in the process of being audited. They were confused and stressed about their next step. Mick, or Michael as he was known in the office, settled them down in his usual professional manner. After a detailed explanation of the process, each person left relieved, graciously thanking him as they ended their appointment.

Mick chuckled at the memory of his boss calling him a superstar. A bit of an exaggeration, but it sure felt good to be recognized as proficient at your job. Hopefully, his hard work will put him closer to his goal of becoming a partner with the firm.

He slid onto the barstool and emitted a long sigh. He was tired, thirsty, and needed some relaxation, but it was hard to unwind with a personal problem weighing on his mind—Reb, how she made him feel. Complicated was the best word to describe his thoughts at the moment.

Mo's was cool and dimly lit. Mick glanced around. Two burly guys sat at one end of the bar, eyes looking straight ahead. Each had a couple of long-necked beer bottles lined up in front of them. Behind him, a bearded man racked balls on a green felted pool table. The jukebox in the corner played a Willie Nelson tune. A completely different vibe than the raucous night crowd.

The bartender, a woman in a tight, low-cut T-shirt, her blonde hair pulled up in a ponytail, was slicing oranges for the garnish tray. She noticed him and smiled cheerfully. "Hey, Mick. Having your usual?"

"Please."

"Hard day at the office?"

"That obvious?"

"It isn't like you to come in this early, especially on a night you aren't singing." She set a frosty bottle of beer on the bar top.

He acknowledged her with a slight nod. "Thanks, Brenda." Mick placed a twenty down on the bar.

"Can I get you anything to eat?"

"Nope, I just needed to unwind for a bit." He lifted the beer to his lips and took a long drink.

She gave him another smile, then returned to slicing the fruit.

"Hey, Brenda!" A man near the pool table yelled. "Turn on the TV. There's a game starting!"

"Sure," she replied matter-of-factly as she wiped her hands on a bar rag. Tossing the towel aside, she reached for the TV remote, clicked the 'On' button, then headed toward the back room.

Mick stared absent mindedly as a local news channel opened on the large screen above the bar.

A pretty, young reporter smiled into the camera, her long auburn hair falling over her shoulders in loose waves. "I'm in downtown Phoenix with Rebecca Prentice, an assistant attorney with the Whittaker Law Firm." She turned to the woman wearing a cream-colored suit. "Good afternoon. Would you prefer I call you Miss Prentice or Rebecca?"

A tight smile crossed the attorney's face. "Rebecca is fine."

Mick's stomach lurched. Reb? He placed his beer on the bar and leaned slightly forward to focus better on the television. He couldn't believe what he was seeing.

"Thank you." The slender reporter brushed a strand of hair behind her ear with her free hand, then shoved the microphone back toward Rebecca. "Would you be kind enough to let our viewers know how the Marlow case is progressing?"

Rebecca turned toward the cameraman, speaking straight to him. "I can assure you that our office is hard at work. At this time, the facts are not all in."

Mick shuddered in disbelief as he stared at the screen. His mind started to spin with questions. What am I seeing? Wait a minute, he thought. Did I hear right? Did she say, assistant attorney?

"So, you see the trial playing out on time?" The reporter asked.

"We don't anticipate any delays, and we're very optimistic the outcome will be in our favor."

"Thank you, Rebecca. I appreciate your time. Oh, and while I have you here, our viewers are curious about your father. Senator Prentice. How is your family holding up through all the divorce proceedings?"

What the hell? He'd known Reb...Rebecca for weeks and hadn't realized who she was. How had that happened? Why hadn't he questioned her last name? She mentioned it was Prentice, but he hadn't given it a second thought. A coincidence was all. Millions of people have the same name.

"I'm not going to comment about a personal matter."

"Will it impact your ability to stay focused?"

"Of course not," Rebecca exclaimed.

"Do you think his affaire will change voter opinions on his platform?"

"We're done here." Rebecca stepped away from the camera's sight.

Mick picked up his beer and drained it. Holy shit, he thought. She's the senator's daughter. What else is she hiding? And, more importantly, why?

The reporter sweetly smiled as Rebecca retreated, then looked into the camera. "There you have it, friends. This is Jordan St. James reporting from channel 10—"

The screen went black momentarily when Brenda switched the local news to a sports channel.

Finished with his beer, Mick slid the bottle back across the bar's surface and signaled for Brenda to bring him another.

"You doing okay?" Brenda asked, sounding concerned.

"I'm fine." He muttered.

She nodded and stepped away, clearly understanding he was in no mood for chit-chat.

Mick sat numbly, staring at the wide screen above the bar, showing two teams battling it out on the basketball court. He lifted the second beer and drained it. As he placed the empty bottle down on the bar, his shoulders stiffened in resolve.

Decision made.

It was past time for Reb to meet the honest Mick. No more excuses and no more delays. He frowned. For better or worse, there was no turning back now. It was time for the truth, no matter the outcome.

And time for her to be honest with him.

#

Mick was a fraud. Oh, sure, he was a musician, that part was true, but he definitely wasn't starving. Not from the article she'd read about him online, now for the third time.

According to this write-up, he should run for bachelor of the year. What a lowdown jerk!

Rebecca leaned back in the kitchen chair. Taking a deep breath, she fought the tears forming again. She couldn't understand what was going on. Why hadn't Mick told her he was a tax accountant for a large firm? Instead, he'd led her to believe he was happily living his life in the music world, enjoying the thrills as they came. Why would he do that? It made no sense.

She stared at his picture. He stood in front of an expensive BMW, precisely like the car he'd shown up in to take her to the symphony, and he'd told her it was a rental.

Hadn't he?

Now she couldn't exactly remember what he'd said. Still, Mick had led her to believe he'd rented it, so what's his game? What could he possibly want from her? Was their entire relationship based on a joke?

Rebecca closed her laptop and reached for a tissue to wipe her tears. The whole Mick thing boggled her mind. So much so that she'd left the office early using the excuse she needed to check on her friend. And it was true. She did want to stop and see Rayna. She was released a short time earlier, and Trisha had taken her home with her.

Making a quick stop by the grocery store, she bought a half-dozen blueberry muffins and headed to Trisha's. Rebecca spent the next hour making every effort to be cheerful as they visited, drank tea, munched on muffins, and then settled Rayna into the guest room. After helping her friend clean the kitchen, Rebecca went straight home.

She thought she'd done an excellent job of hiding her shock at finding Mick's identity from her friends, but now in the safety of her kitchen, she let her emotions flow. She dabbed at her eyes, blew her nose, and then tossed the tissue toward the trash basket. She missed it again. Used tissues were beginning to pile up on the floor.

She glanced around and sniffed the air. Something smelled bad. "Oh, no!" Burning tomato sauce. Dinner! Realizing what was happening in her kitchen, she jumped from her chair and quickly rushed toward the stove. She'd forgotten about the leftover pasta she was warming in her misery. Turning off the burners, she stared at the bubbling spaghetti, which now had formed a blackened crust around the edge of the pan. She gagged, seeing the unsightly mess.

In disgust, she turned to the sink and dumped the scorched blob into the garbage disposal. Oh, who cares, she thought, I'm not hungry anyway.

Sucking in a deep breath, she headed to the refrigerator, retrieved a bottle of wine, then poured herself a generous glass.

She had downed her second refill and was about to head to bed when she heard a knock at the front door. She thought about ignoring it for a moment, but maybe it was one of her friends or a neighbor needing something.

She opened the door enough to peek out. She frowned. Mick.

"What do you want?" she snarled.

He blinked. "May I come in?"

She hesitated.

"Please," he added.

She shrugged, then stepped aside to let the door swing open enough for him to enter. She pointed her finger toward his chest when he closed the door behind him and yelled, "You are a lying sack of crap!"

Mick's eyes widened at her outburst. He took a step backward but didn't speak.

"You failed to mention you're a tax attorney in a big firm. All this time, you've been lying to me. So, what else haven't you told me, Mick, if that's your name? Is it?"

"Yes, sometimes—"

"Don't bother." She cut him off. "I don't want to know. I don't care anymore." She glanced toward the floor.

"I understand what you're feeling. I—"

Her head shot up, and she caught his gaze. "Don't! Don't tell me you understand my feelings because you have no idea."

Not knowing what to say, she crossed the room to the sofa and flopped down. Shaking her head, she stared at him, trying to understand what was happening. He'd lied about being a full-time musician. She'd got him a job singing at her parents' party. She'd offered him money! She wanted to help him get a music career going. Oh, sure, he'd turned down the money, but maybe that was part of his plan. Earn her trust, and she'd offer him more? How often had her office represented a woman scammed of her life savings by her supposedly wonderful boyfriend? How could she be so gullible? She slapped both hands on the couch.

"I never meant to deceive you." He lowered himself into the chair across from her.

"But you did."

"I wanted you to like me, and I wanted to show you a different lifestyle."

"Well, you did that all right. You showed me a life with a fraud."

"Reb, would you have given me a chance if you thought I was like every guy you knew?"

"We'll never know now, will we?" She reached for the tissue box on the coffee table.

"I can't tell you how many times I wanted to tell you who I was, but I got scared every time I started to. Scared you'd see me differently, and I'd be boring to you."

"Do you see me as someone that superficial? Someone who couldn't like a man who works hard to be a success?" She tossed the tissue box aside, reached for the decorative pillow next to her then hugged it to her chest. "Wow. Just wow."

"I wanted to be the exciting guy."

"You need to go now, Mick. I mean Michael. I need some time."

He nodded and stood. Without a word, he headed toward the door. Before he stepped outside, he hesitated, then glanced back, his expression serious. "I love you. That's the truth."

Her eyes stung.

He crossed the threshold, stopped, and turned slightly. "You know, you lied to me as well, Rebecca. You give a nice interview, Miss assistant attorney." Then he closed the door behind him.

Reb jumped up from the couch and ran to the window. He saw me on TV! He's right; I haven't been entirely truthful. But what I did was different. I wanted to spare his feelings. I was being nice. He was being deceitful.

Tears slid down her cheeks as she peeked through the blinds to watch him walk down the driveway. He stopped momentarily and glanced toward the front door. The entry light from her porch shone across his face. He wasn't smiling, and for a split second, she thought he would turn around and come back.

He didn't.

Mick got onto his motorcycle and backed out of her driveway.

"Should I run after him? No. He won't go. He'll change his mind," she argued aloud.

Mick drove away without a glance in her direction, leaving her staring through the glass, feeling completely alone.

Chapter Fifteen

The Arizona late afternoon weather conditions couldn't have been more ideal for a party. Seventy-eight degrees and sunny with a slight breeze. The renewal ceremony started at sunset, so the photographer had asked the family to arrive by four-thirty, assuring them that was plenty of time to take pictures before their guests arrived.

Rebecca and her mother were in a luxurious suite at the country club dedicated as a bridal or a special event dressing room. Her mother sat on a plush stool in front of a mirror, her hands trembling with excitement as she attempted to pin a spray of flowers into her French Twist hairstyle.

"Here, mom, let me help." Rebecca moved to her mother's side and quickly secured the flowers. "There. You look beautiful."

Olivia beamed. "Thank you."

Rebecca bent down and put her cheek next to her mother's. They smiled into the mirror as they studied each other's reflections.

"Look how pretty we look." Her mother reached up and lightly touched Rebecca's chin. "Thank you, darling, for helping me with this party. I couldn't have done it alone."

"Oh, Mom. Don't make me cry and ruin my makeup."

"No. We'll save our happy tears for the ceremony." Her mother stood and ran her hands along the side of her dress. A lovely tea-length, cream chiffon lace with a scoop neckline and a long-sleeved lace jacket. "Well, this is as good as I'm going to look, so let's find your father and take our pictures."

Rebecca glanced once more into the mirror and fluffed her hair with her fingers. Her mother had helped to select the perfect outfit, a sleek and sexy dress in periwinkle blue. The soft crepe fabric fell below her knees, and a long side split showed off one of her long legs. A sprinkle of sequins accented the tie straps. Her only jewelry were Tiffany diamond drop earrings and her favorite diamond bracelet.

Satisfied with her appearance, she glanced at the gold-framed clock on the wall and then told her mom, "You go find dad. I'll check to ensure the flowers have arrived, then meet you near the first photo site."

They gave each other a final hug before heading their separate ways.

Rebecca entered the clubhouse and nodded appreciatively. The staff beautifully decorated the party room in soft peach and ivory colors that flowed out onto the vast, covered courtyard. Outside white chairs were placed in neat rows facing a small table covered with white fabric, and a vase overflowing with peach and white roses graced the center. In front of the table was where her parents would stand and recite their vows.

Pleased with the outdoor seating arrangement, Rebecca stepped back into the party room and gave a white-jacketed waiter, who was placing crystal flutes on tables, a thumbs-up and a wide smile. As she started to leave to join her parents and the photographer, the band guys walked in and began to set up in the corner. Her smile faded.

The group came highly recommended by the country club, and Rebecca had no doubts they could entertain the guests, still... A moment of sadness hit when reminded that Mick would not be the one singing her parents' favorite tunes.

It had been three weeks since Mick walked out of her condo, and somehow, she'd managed not to break down and cry for the past five days. She was getting better. Of course, some moments brought heartache. Like when she heard a specific song on the car radio or caught the familiar scent of an aftershave that Mick wore, or now as she watched the band setting up. She closed her eyes, attempting to fight back the rising tears. She couldn't break down today. She heaved a sigh, blinked, then forced another smile. She would not dampen the evening with her petty personal problem. Tonight belonged to her mother and father. She would act as the perfect daughter and do them proud.

Thirty minutes later, as the photographer snapped multiple photos, Rebecca's smile was truly radiant. She posed happily with her parents in various locations selected for ideal pictures and had no doubts they would turn out fantastic. And best of all, she hadn't thought about Mick once during the shoot. Well, maybe once, as the evening breeze swept across her shoulders and jogged the memory of his lips brushing her skin, causing her eyes to drift closed.

"Open your eyes, Rebecca, and smile for us again," The photographer instructed.

Startled by his words, her eyes shot open. She blinked. "Sorry."

Regaining her composure, she leaned nearer to her parents as the camera clicked a few more times.

Finally freed from the photo shoot, Rebecca returned to the clubhouse.

The party was only an intimate get-together of their closest friends, and Rebecca became the perfect hostess as the guests began to arrive. She greeted everyone with a warm smile and affectionately offered small talk, making sure each guest felt special.

Since everyone attending already knew each other, and most had been friends for years, Rebecca's job of being a good hostess was easy. Although, making people feel comfortable was something she was good at anyway. After all, she'd been brought up in a world of entertaining family, friends, and strangers alike. The brilliant daughter raised in a political family by a father who expected perfection. Intelligent, reliable, and beautiful. Those were the words she heard quite often from her father.

I wonder what it would be like to hear the words wild child from him when describing me. She giggled. Rebecca's thoughts quickly disappeared when Rayna walked in holding hands with Dr. Cooper. Her face glowed with a newly fallen-in-love smile. The handsome doctor seemed smitten as well. He stepped close beside her, guiding her into the room.

Rayna looked stunning, dressed in vibrant pink. A sheer skirt fell to her ankles, partially hiding the ugly boot her podiatrist still made her wear. Even with an injured foot, she walked in like a supermodel. Pink hair, a softer shade than her skirt, brushed her shoulders in loose waves, emphasizing her high cheekbones. As usual, she radiated confidence.

"Rayna, you are beautiful. I'm so glad you're here."

"I wouldn't miss it. Your mom and dad are like my second parents. Oh, you remember Zach?" Rayna's eyes sparkled as she glanced from Rebecca to Zack and then back again. "Doctor Cooper, from the hospital."

"Of course." Rebecca offered her hand. "Nice to see you again, Doctor Cooper."

"My pleasure." A dimple flashed on his right cheek as he accepted her offered hand. "Please, call me Zach."

Rebecca could easily see what Rayna saw in Doctor Cooper...er...Zach. The first word that popped into her mind was captivating. Lord knows Rayna always did like a smooth talker. But Heaven help him if he breaks her heart. He'll have the wrath of Scarlett and Trisha, not to mention me, to deal with if he does. I know firsthand how bad a broken heart hurts.

She showed Zach her sweetest rehearsed smile. "Welcome, Zach."

"Oh, good. Scarlett and David are here," Rayna announced.

Rebecca turned to see Scarlett and her friend, David, step through the doorway. Scarlett looked beautiful, dressed in a pastel print sheath that hugged her hips perfectly. Silver hoops dangled from her ears, and multi-colored bracelets layered together graced one arm. Her bare shoulders sparkled with a dusting of glitter, only to be out-shown by her silver and rhinestone high-heeled sandals. David was equally handsome in a tailored western-style suit and snakeskin boots. Rebecca mentally shook her head and thought, what a pair.

Rebecca greeted Scarlett with a hug and told David how nice it was to see him again.

"My pleasure to be included," David said.

Scarlett grabbed Rebecca's hands and exclaimed, "Everything is beautiful. You've done an amazing job."

"Thank you. I hope everyone has a good time tonight."

"I know we will," Scarlett answered as she leaned toward her date.

"Go ahead and sit down. Rayna should get off her foot, and I need to check on my dad." Rebecca pointed to the nearby table for six. "Trisha should be here anytime and can join you."

Rebecca glanced around the room as her friends settled themselves at the table. While she had briefly visited with her friends, more guests had filtered in, and she found her dad standing near the entrance surrounded by people. He looked splendid in his suit. Tailored for him in the perfect shade of deep grey, accompanied by a peach-colored tie that brought out the silver in his hair. He was indeed a magnificent-looking older man. Oh, dad, I can see why you can easily charm everyone.

He spotted her walking his way. Rebecca watched as he politely excused himself from his friends and stepped toward her. "Here you are, Princess. Having a good time?" Taking her hand, he squeezed it affectionately.

"I am."

"Good." He guided her to a quiet corner of the room out of earshot of their guests. "I have to admit I'm a little nervous."

"About...?"

"Reciting my vows. I wrote them myself and I don't want to sound fake. I want your mother to trust my sincerity." He raised an eyebrow as if hoping she'd give him advice.

"I don't believe this, Dad. You worried about speaking and sounding honest?" She couldn't hold back a giggle. "I'm sorry. I don't mean to make light of your feelings, and it's just you give speeches all the time. You have always been honest in your opinions, which is why you're so well respected."

"I wasn't always honest with Olivia," he confessed.

"She's forgiven you."

"I'm not sure I'll ever forgive myself." He took a deep breath, preparing himself for whatever she might say.

Rebecca stared at her father. It took a second for his words to sink in. How did she respond to a man bearing his soul to her? "Oh, Daddy." She stepped forward and embraced him. "Tell mom how you feel. Everything will be all right."

As she held her father, she realized she barely knew him. Not the real man inside his larger-than-life persona. He'd always been the one who took care of her. He always had the answers she needed. He fixed anything she asked of him without hesitation. Maybe he needed to be taken care of occasionally.

"I'm sorry," Rebecca whispered.

"Sorry for what? You've nothing to be sorry about. You are my brilliant, perfect girl. I'm so proud of you."

Rebecca reached up and kissed her father's cheek. "Thanks, Dad."

"Enough about me. What do you say we get a drink? I could use a strong bourbon right now."

"Good idea." Rebecca guided her dad toward the bar. "Grab yourself a drink. While you do that, I'll go check on mom."

"Okay, darling."

As Frank motioned to the bartender, Rebecca left him to continue her search for her mother. Finally, Rebecca found Olivia in the ladies' room playing with her makeup. "Here you are, mom."

Olivia withdrew a lipstick from her purse and applied it lightly. "Oh, Rebecca, I'm so nervous. Why did I think this was a good idea?" She dropped the lipstick back into her purse and then blotted her lips with a tissue.

"What do you mean? Don't you want to remarry dad?"

"Of course I do. It's just that saying the words in front of our friends has me trembling."

"You? Nothing makes you panic."

"This has. I mean, at our age, trying to act like newlyweds. For goodness's sake."

"Mom, all your friends want to show their support. This party is for them as much as it is for you and dad. It's a night to celebrate love. Old and new."

"You're right. Our dearest friends are all here."

"Yes. They certainly are."

"I'm not being foolish, am I.? Expecting things to go on as if nothing ever happened?"

"Mom, you know I want my parents together." She reached over and brushed a stray hair off her mother's cheek. "I suppose all kids want that, but it's something only you and dad can make happen."

She met Rebecca's gaze. "I do love him. I always have."

"Well, I know he loves you. He's sorry for being such a fool."

"Men can be foolish from time to time."

"Even the best of them." Rebecca sighed. "Why do you think dad did it, mom? Cheat on you." She blinked. Had she crossed a line by asking a personal question about her father?

Her mother didn't hesitate with her answer. "Because he's human. He was scared. Scared of losing his status in the community. Not getting re-elected. Letting his family down. Mostly of getting old. Men are silly that way."

Clearing her throat, Rebecca admitted, "I'm sorry, dad hurt you."

No one spoke for several seconds.

Then she reached for Rebeca's hands and confessed while holding them tightly. "I hurt him too. I pushed. I made him feel obligated to do more, have more, and be more. I was so caught up with my social events that I didn't notice he was tired. He was losing his enthusiasm for life. It was easy for a pretty, young woman to turn his head with a little flattery."

Rebecca found herself asking, "Do you feel that someday you'll think about what he did? Maybe have second thoughts about forgiving him?"

Rebecca's mother pressed her lips together for a moment, then answered, her voice strong and steady. "I think we'll be much too busy planning our next adventure to dwell over any past mistakes."

Rebecca took in a huge breath, then blew it out slowly. She stared at the woman standing before her, so pretty and nervous because she was about to remarry the same man she'd lived with for almost forty years. It suddenly dawned on her how lucky she was to have such wonderful loving people as her parents. Whatever else might be going on in her life, this was something she'd forever be grateful for and never take lightly again.

"Let's go get you and daddy married. And lucky me. I get to be present this time."

They were laughing as they left the ladies' room.

Chapter Sixteen

The afternoon sun slipped below the tall canopy of trees shading the golf course, sending rays of light into the silver strands of her father's hair. Rebecca's heart filled with love as she watched this elegant man gaze into her mother's eyes and whisper, "Are you ready to marry me again?"

A smile tugged at the corners of her mother's mouth, then she answered, "I am."

Soft romantic music began to play in the background. Rebecca took the long-stemmed peach rose her mother held, kissed her on the cheek, then scooted into the chair directly in front of her parents. She blinked back a tear as her parents faced each other, holding hands and smiling.

Several seconds passed.

Rebecca glanced down at the rose she gripped, realizing her palms were sweating. How silly, she thought. No reason for me to be nervous.

Glancing to her left, Rebecca caught the eye of Scarlett, who smiled and nodded. Then directly behind Scarlett to Rayna, who also gave her a reassuring smile. Trisha and her date had arrived and taken the seats next to Rayna and Zach. Rebecca nodded in acknowledgment, then turned back to her parents.

The patio area grew quiet.

Finally, her father broke the silence. "Olivia and I want to thank you all for being with us this evening. As we pledge our love to each other for a second time, it's even more special to be in the presence of our beloved friends and family."

Rebecca offered them both an approving smile.

He winked, then turned to face her mother once more. He cleared his throat, then spoke softly, "I, Frank Prentice, love you today as much as I did when we first stood like this before our family and friends."

Rebecca blinked back a tear. They are so sweet.

Her mother spoke. "I, Olivia Prentice, promise to still love you, for better or worse, forever."

Frank added to his vows. "I never imagined I could face the possibility of losing you. I am beyond grateful that I get to keep you by my side, and I promise to honor you and love you for the rest of my life."

Something happened as Rebecca listened to her mother and father speak their vows. After all these years, the disappointments, the betrayals, the hurt, they still forgave each other and loved with a passion that nothing could break.

"I promise you the same, Frank." Olivia looked into his eyes and continued, "Always and forever."

As she watched her parents gaze into each other's eyes, Rebecca remembered how not so long ago, she'd looked at Mick in the same way. So, lovingly and trusting, but that was before she knew the real Mick. Why couldn't she put that stupid, lying, arrogant, unforgivable Mick out of her mind? She was sorry she ever laid eyes on him. Wasn't she? Darn, why did hating him so much hurt so badly?

Her parents sealed their vows with a kiss as their friends clapped and cheered.

Rebecca gave her full attention to her parents as they turned toward their audience and smiled.

"Thank you all so much for your love and support. Now, head back inside, everyone, dinner is being served, and the bar is open. Go enjoy!" More cheers and applause followed her father's words.

Within ten minutes, everyone returned to the party room, where the staff was serving the food. Rebecca greeted Trisha with a big hug, then ushered her and her date Jason to the table where Scarlett and Rayna were already seated. After a few minutes of small talk, Rebecca excused herself to go sit with her parents.

Dinner was delicious. The club's chef outdid himself. He'd created the tastiest choices of Prime Rib beef or a delicate herb-crusted roast chicken. By her third glass of champagne, Rebecca felt quite proud of herself. She'd managed to be the perfect hostess, given a lovely toast to her parents, and smiled and laughed all evening.

Up until the band she'd hired for the night started playing one of her favorites that Mick sang at Mo's bar. Hurt flooded her heart once more. What if, she thought. What if I'd been truthful? What if he hadn't lied to me? What if…what if?

He'd blown it with Reb. Mick slammed his hand on the car's steering wheel. He'd blown it with the one woman who'd stolen his heart. What in the world made him think that leading her to believe he was a struggling, song writing, part-time biker bar singer was an excellent way to make her like him?

Damn it!

Mick pulled into the driveway of his two-story, North Scottsdale townhome. It had been a long night at Mo's. Especially after a full eight-hour day with clients at the office. He'd barely had time to get out of his suit and change into jeans by the time the band started their first song. It had worked out. The crowd thought his late entrance was on purpose.

Sitting in with the band had always relaxed him, but tonight the crowd at Mo's had been extra rowdy. They had kept requesting hard rock songs. He rubbed a weary hand across the back of his neck, then pushed the garage door opener. Right now, all he wanted to do was take a shower, hit the sheets, and forget about everything. Forget all the work stress, Mo's, and Reb.

If only that were possible. There was no forgetting Reb. But then again, she'd lied to him as well. Did she think that little of him? Obviously, she hadn't planned to keep him in her life for long, he was only entertainment and a fun guy to have around temporarily.

Mick pulled into the garage and killed the engine. A few minutes later, he hit the light in his kitchen, tossed his keys on the counter, and headed straight to the refrigerator. His eyes roamed the shelves looking for something tasty. His inventory included leftover pizza, a carton of eggs, a bottle of ketchup, a six-pack of beer, and a jug of 2 percent milk. Nothing looked worth the trouble of either heating it up or taking the time to prepare.

Should've picked up a burger on the way home, he thought.

Grabbing the milk, he closed the refrigerator door, poured himself a glass, and drank it while leaning against the sink. Feeling slightly better, he marched toward the bedroom and his welcoming bed. But first, he needed a relaxing hot shower.

Minutes later, Mick threw his head back to let the hot water stream across his face, then turned and let it pound across his shoulders as he ran a soapy washcloth over his chest. Reb, he thought. If it were only as easy to forget you as it is to wash off the dirt and stale cigarette smoke from Mo's.

Finished with the shower, Mick toweled himself off and headed back into the bedroom. Too tired to get into a pair of pajamas, he slid, naked, under the covers. Letting out a long sigh, he reached for the lamp on the nightstand and turned it off. Darkness filled the room, Mick closed his eyes, but his brain stayed active. Thoughts of Reb treaded through his mind.

Mick remembered the first time he'd taken her into his arms. It was on the dance floor at Mo's. She was there with her friends, sitting in the corner, drinking shots and beer. Someone had asked the owner to have Mick dedicate a song to her and something that would make her feel special. A request like this was nothing new for him. Customers often asked him to sing or play a favorite song for a friend.

He'd assumed the pretty blonde was going through a breakup or maybe just having a bad day, but as she'd taken his hand and pulled her to him on the dance floor, it was as if destiny had taken over. He found himself falling in love. Of course, that would be ridiculous, and nobody falls in love the first time they meet on a dance floor in a crowded biker bar like Mo's.

Still, people do fall in love at first sight. Perhaps he could make her realize there was something real between them. All he needed was another chance. His mind began to race with ideas. Maybe tomorrow night, show up at her doorstep with a dozen roses—too ordinary—or how about with a brass band—definitely wild, but she'd hate disturbing her neighbors.

How about sweeping her away on a hot-air balloon ride? Champagne at dawn? Scoop her up and throw her over the back of a horse? Or better yet, bring the guys from the band to her house. Two or three songs, and she'd invite him in to keep them from upsetting the neighborhood. Then, well, he'd see. He'd think of a way…tomorrow. Smiling, Mick rolled over onto his stomach and let sleep come.

Chapter Seventeen

Enough already. A nagging voice inside Rebecca's head urged her to get out from under the covers and quit thinking about Mick. She opened her eyes and glanced toward her bedroom window. Morning sunshine streamed through the half-closed shutters. She'd been up once already, trudged into the kitchen, started the morning coffee, then crawled back into bed while waiting for it to brew.

No reason to be up too early. It wasn't a workday. Then she remembered she'd promised her parents she'd meet them for brunch. Darn it. I won't be able to sleep all day.

Usually, she'd have begged off getting together with them since their renewal of vows party had lasted late into the night. Her feet hurt from dancing, and her head hurt from all the champagne, but they'd insisted on a late breakfast or early lunch.

"We have things to go over with you before we leave for the airport," they had stated.

Fine, she finally agreed they were right. Brunch it is.

Since she planned to stay at their place while they sailed off on a second honeymoon cruise to the Bahamas, Rebecca did need a refresher course about a few things. Such as how the remote worked for their new flat-screen TV. What day the garbage should be taken out. When the landscaper came, if she should pay him, and if so, how much. And, of course, the main reason she would stay at their house was to feed her mom's twelve-year-old poodle named Zoey. She'd need to make a to-do list. List! There's that flippin' word again. She groaned, threw back the covers, and padded barefoot toward the kitchen.

Twenty minutes later, she trekked toward the shower, turned on the taps, stripped off her pajamas, and stepped under the hot spray. Lathering herself with sweet-smelling body soap and leaning under the showerhead, she imagined the water washing away all her troubles along with the foaming suds. Slowly, as the water pounded the back of her neck and across her shoulders, she began to feel better, as if she was back in control of her thoughts.

I better get a move on, Rebecca decided as she wrapped herself in a fluffy robe and exited the bathroom. The morning was getting away from her, and she hoped to have enough time to stop by the women's shelter before going to her parents. She had a large box of donations to drop off. Items she knew would be greatly appreciated.

After quickly putting on her favorite jeans and a loose-fitting shirt, she checked herself in the bathroom mirror, applied lipstick and mascara, brushed her hair, and smiled. Good enough. Minutes later, she'd loaded her car and was headed to the shelter.

By the time she'd dropped off the donations and reached her parent's elegant ranch house, the one she'd grown up in, it was getting close to eleven. She parked her car in the wide circular driveway, then sprinted up the brick stairway leading to the front entry.

A memory hit her as she hurried to the door. She had made this dash many times in her younger years. She remembered always running, always in a hurry to get home from somewhere. She was either hanging out with a study group or an after-school sports event. Finding the door unlocked, Rebecca flung it open and yelled, "I'm here."

"Ready for a mimosa?" her father asked as he stepped from the kitchen. He carried two stemmed glasses and handed her one without waiting for her answer.

"Thanks, Dad."

"Your mother is in the kitchen making crepes. Better get in there before we have to open a restaurant to get rid of them all. You'd think she was feeding an army." He leaned in to kiss her cheek.

"Go big or go home. That's mom."

"I'd certainly be much bigger if I let her feed me all my meals." He patted his stomach with his free hand.

"I can hear you," her mother scolded from the hallway. "Good morning, Sweetheart."

"Hi, Mom. Yum, something smells good."

"All your favorites. Grab a plate. We're set up in the dining room."

Rebecca slid into her regular place at the table as her mother served her two of the crepes. "These look delicious, Mom."

"Thank you, darling. Would you like strawberries and whipped cream?" She placed a bowl of bright red berries in front of Rebecca, "And you must have some of your dad's peppers and scrambled eggs."

"Didn't you two have anything better to do this morning other than cook? Like pack?" Rebecca asked as she spooned strawberries onto her crepes.

"Oh, pish posh, we've been packed for days. And you know how much your dad likes to cook. Besides, he's retired now and has nothing else to do."

"He's only been retired two weeks." She reached for the can of whipped cream.

"Well, that's two weeks of him doing nothing." She turned to her husband. "I'm not about to let you sit around and get stale."

"I have plenty to do around here. And I've been thinking about new hobbies, plus I'll start playing more golf." Her father placed a platter of eggs on the table, then took a seat.

"What about you, Rebecca?" Her mother leaned closer while changing the subject. "Fill us in on what you've been doing. Besides work."

"Besides work, nothing special." Rebecca didn't meet her mother's questioning look. She only shrugged and scooped eggs onto her plate.

"Not according to Scarlett. The other day she mentioned you've been seeing someone special. Is that right?"

"Scarlett is mistaken. There's no one in my life at the moment."

Ignoring her daughter's denial, she continued, "Scarlett said someone in a band." She tilted her head toward Rebecca. "Why didn't you invite him to our party?"

Rebecca shrugged. "It wasn't an option."

"What's this?" Her father questioned. "A musician messing with your feelings? Do I need to have my boys pay him a visit?"

"Your boys? You don't have any boys." Rebecca couldn't contain her laughter.

"Ignore your father. He's been binge-watching too many mafia TV shows."

Her father waved aside her mother's comment. "Don't underestimate this old man."

"I do have something I'd like to run by you." This seemed like a good time to change the subject, especially since she didn't want her mother to keep questioning her about Mick. "I'm hoping you have connections who might know someone who could offer some help."

"Let's hear about it." Her father set down his fork and pushed his plate back, giving Rebecca his full attention.

"The charity I support. I've mentioned Haven of Peace to you before." Rebecca took a deep breath and then continued. "The place that gives temporary housing to women recovering from abused relationships. Or, simply due to circumstances out of their control, they have found themselves homeless. The problem is that it's becoming overcrowded, so they desperately need to expand." Rebecca frowned. "It seems more and more women are in trouble. It's mind-boggling how bad it's getting."

"Do you know what they have in mind?" her father replied

"One solution is moving to a larger place or perhaps acquiring a second home. However, the problem is there's no funding to do either." Rebecca shrugged. "Haven is a non-profit organization; unfortunately, they're running out of money."

"That is quite a problem." He frowned.

"Rebecca," her mother said. "I've worked on many successful fund-raising events back in the day. You've helped me as well. When we get home from this cruise, let's put our heads together and toss around some ideas. Perhaps we can come up with a solution."

"And of course," her father stated, "we'll make a nice donation to your cause. I'm sure I can also get some of the fellows at the country club interested."

"Wow, thank you both so much. I wish I had more time to help. Those women need assistance, but things are hectic at the law office. I've had to push my volunteering efforts to the back burner. There's just not enough time in the day." Not to mention getting sidetracked with Mick. She took a deep breath. No, she wasn't about to bring up his name; he was her past.

"All right, darling." Her mother glanced at her watch, then stood and began clearing the table. "I have a lot to go over with you this morning. But don't worry, I've written it all down, so you won't forget."

"Right, Mom." Great. The dreaded 'L' word.

# # #

"I have the list right here in front of me," Mick spoke clearly into his phone. "Yes, I'll have the reports ready for you by Monday morning. No problem." He hung up, leaned back on his oversized couch, and hit the remote to the TV. He mindlessly channel-surfed, hoping something interesting on Saturday programming would catch his attention. He glanced at his watch. The sports event he planned to see today didn't start for another hour.

Mick popped the top on his beer can and took a long drink. He'd had a restless night's sleep. He couldn't stop thinking about Reb. He recalled that last night was the date of her parent's renewal of vows party, the one he'd been invited to sing at before he and Reb had their fight. Wonder how that went? Did she hire another singer, or only use a DJ? Well, it didn't matter, whoever or whatever, it hadn't been him.

For a brief second, he wanted to pick up his phone and call her. He could casually ask how the party had gone, then see if maybe she'd like to come to Mo's tonight and hear him sing. It couldn't hurt to ask. He glanced at his phone, and it was right there on the coffee table within reach. But no, she wouldn't want to, and he couldn't bear hearing her rejection. He ran his hand across his face. He needed to shave but had no reason to at the moment. He would later before he headed out for the night.

He took another gulp of beer. He had time to work on Monday's tax reports before the game started, but there was no rush. The goal for today was to drink beer and watch sports until time to head to Mo's. After all, it was Saturday, and Monday was a long time away. He'd work on them tomorrow.

The career he'd always enjoyed was becoming stressful. He didn't seem to have the same drive anymore. Becoming a partner in the firm was losing its thrill. Lately, his mind focused more on his music—and Reb. He only saw musical notes or Reb's face whenever he tried to work with numbers. He felt as if he was being pulled in different directions. Mick frowned. For the first time in as long as he could remember, he had no definite plan for his life. He felt lost and depressed. And he didn't like it. "Suck it up dude," he muttered. "You did this to yourself."

Closing his eyes, he let his thoughts drift to Reb once more. He remembered the feel of her velvety lips, her slender body curved perfectly into his, and the sweet smell of her perfume as he ran his hands through her soft, silky hair. Her tattoo, the pretty colors of blues and greens, swirling together in the shape of a butterfly. He blinked, straightened, groaned, and took another long swig of beer.

He glanced toward his phone again. Taking a deep breath, he reached for it, and without hesitation, he punched Reb's number. Before the call connected, he hit cancel.

Chapter Eighteen

Life goes on.

Two weeks since the renewal of the vows party and three weeks with no attempt from Mick. She'd expected him to put forth some effort and show her he seriously wanted to talk. Was that unrealistic? She shook her head in exasperation. Oh, heck, maybe she should call block him. Then she'd have no reason to keep checking her phone. She sighed.

Thursday night was Rebecca's regular happy hour at the Ritz with her girlfriends. And after giving the idea considerable thought, she decided to go, hoping a night out would take her mind off Mick. She was still at her parent's house while they cruised the Bahamas, and her only companion was Zoey. Since her mom's dog seemed indifferent to anything she had to say, she figured she might as well go out and enjoy herself with her friends.

Rebecca pulled on her jeans, adjusted her shirt, stepped into a pair of heels, then checked herself in the mirror. She'd brushed her hair, letting the waves fall over her shoulders in her favorite style. Not bad.

Grabbing her purse, she hurried out the door, hopped into her car, and headed to the Ritz.

The drive to the downtown bar wasn't long, and she was sitting at the usual table before the sun set. Rebecca's friend Scarlett was already there.

"I've missed getting together," Rebecca told Scarlett. "Especially these butterscotch martinis." She picked up her martini and took a sip. "Yum, and no one makes a cocktail like a bartender at the Ritz."

Scarlett gazed around the room with a sympathetic look in her eyes. "This is where you belong, Rebecca. Here, in a nice place with all the friends who love you. Not in a sleazy bar like Mo's."

"Oh, Scarlett, no, don't be judgmental." Rebecca blurted. "I'm sure the people at Mo's are nice." She sighed, then added, "Not everyone is shady. I mean who stretches the truth more than politicians and lawyers?" With a tilt of her head, Rebecca laughed, then arched her eyebrows. "I should know."

"I'm just trying to make you feel better. I realize you're having a hard time getting over Mick."

"It's okay." Rebecca covered her friend's hand with her own. "I understand you mean well."

At that moment, Rayna entered the restaurant and hurried toward them. She walked without the bulky black boot, and

Rebecca noticed she barely favored her leg. Giving both girls a warm smile, Rayna seated herself at their table. But before speaking, Trisha rushed in and settled herself in the empty chair next to Rebecca.

Soon all of them had drinks on the table. Lifting their glasses, they spoke a toast in unison. "To another great night."

"And to no one going to jail," Scarlett added.

"I'll drink to that," Trisha said as their glasses clinked together.

All four of them burst into laughter. Then soon, the girls were chatting, giggling, and teasing each other with stories from the past as the cocktails flowed.

After the third round of drinks, Trisha asked, "Should we go to a different bar tonight?"

Rebecca winced. "As long as it's not Mo's."

Scarlett's eyebrows rose. "Oh, no, we wouldn't ask you to go there. We know you don't want to run into Mick."

Rayna added, "Absolutely not. I might have to punch him in the face for breaking your heart. The lying skunk."

Rebecca pressed her lips together to keep them from trembling. Then for some reason, she felt the need to defend Mick. "Look, I'll admit I fell hard for the guy, but he lied to me." She shook her head slowly. "How does one forget about that?"

"I know he did, Rebecca." Trisha leaned closer and nodded, "but remember, you weren't exactly truthful with him either."

"I wasn't being deceitful," Rebecca answered abruptly. "I was being nice. There's a difference. I didn't want to make him feel uncomfortable. You know, like he'd have to try and impress me. After all, that's why I went to Mo's semi-disguised in the first place. I didn't want anyone to recognize the senator's daughter in a biker bar. My picture could have ended up on social media or perhaps the national news." Her words continued to swirl around in her brain. She'd had this conversation with herself before. And she was justified in what she did, wasn't she?

"You miss him, don't you?" Trisha asked gently.

Rebecca sucked in a steading breath. "I...I guess I do. But" Rebecca felt tears rising. There was no point trying to convince her friends she didn't miss Mick. They knew her too well and would see through any words of denial she'd offer. And even though it was true she missed him, she couldn't get over being the target of a lie.

Still, she knew in her heart she'd also held back the truth from him. Maybe it would have been better to listen to what he had to say instead of throwing him out without a chance to make his case. He told her that he'd done what he thought she'd wanted.

180

Honestly, could she have led him to believe that?

Rebecca picked at the diamond bracelet on her wrist. As she breathed a sigh as thoughts rumbled through her mind. After all, didn't everyone have the right to prove their innocence? Even if the facts all point to a person as guilty, he should be allowed to tell his side of the story. That's only fair. I wish—

"Rebecca?" Trisha patted her arm, bringing her back to the present.

"Hum. What?" Rebecca glanced around to see all her friends staring at her.

"You seemed to have drifted off." Scarlett added, "Do you want to talk about it?"

"No. No, there's nothing to say." Rebecca lifted her drink and took a sip. "But thanks anyway."

"Look, you can't end it the way you did with Mick," Trisha stated.

Rayna and Scarlett both shot her a warning look, but Trisha waved them off and continued. "True, I agree with Rayna. He acted like a jerk. And maybe he truly is one, but you need to talk to him. Explain how you feel. Then you can rationally decide if it's over between the two of you. Remember, there are three sides to a story. His, hers, and the truth. At least that's what you've always told us." Trisha glanced toward the others, looking for confirmation.

Rayna and Scarlett both nodded.

Rebecca ran a finger over the rim of her martini glass. She appreciated her friend's viewpoint, but it didn't make her feel better. Actually, she felt worse.

Was it possible she had been the one who hadn't acted rationally? Perhaps the adult thing to do would be to listen to him state his case. Of course, it didn't mean she automatically needed to forgive him. She'd only allow him to present his side and then let him hear hers calmly and rationally. At least that way, she could make an accurate decision based on facts, not one decided from an emotional state. After all, that's what she did daily at her job; research and listen to points as they were presented.

Rebecca's mouth quivered. Then hoping it wasn't the alcohol talking and this wouldn't be a terrible mistake, she said, "All right, call an Uber. Let's go to Mo's."

#

It was late evening when Mick pulled into Mo's crowded parking lot. He eased his bike into a slot near the back door and killed the rumbling engine. He kicked the stand and swung off. As he was about to open the entrance door, the pungent perfume of a nearby female assaulted his nose. She moved next to him and ran her long fingernails across his arm.

"Hey, handsome." Her voice, soft and seductive, whispered close to his ear. "You alone tonight?"

"Looks that way, Darlene." He offered her a smile.

"Buy me a drink?" Her dark eyelashes fluttered.

"Sure." He opened the door and stood back, allowing Darlene to enter first, then he followed her inside the bar.

Mick had met Darlene when he first joined the band. She was a regular customer at Mo's and pleasant enough. He'd dated her more than once, but nothing serious came from it. Darlene wasn't the settling-on-one-guy type, which worked perfectly for Mick. She had no expectations for a relationship. As it turned out, they made better friends than lovers.

As usual, she looked hot tonight. He couldn't help but notice. She wore tight-fitting black jeans, high-heeled boots, and a top that stretched across her bust, giving him a clear view of her ample curves. She'd brushed her long red hair into loose curls that fell over her shoulders. Yeah, he'd buy Darlene a drink.

He nodded to Henry, the bouncer, as he walked Darlene toward the bar area. Henry nodded and gave Mick a thumbs-up while letting out a low chuckle. Mick shook his head in reply, trying to get across the fact he was merely being a nice guy and buying the lady a drink. Henry's response was a shrug.

When he had her settled on a stool near the far end of the horseshoe, curved bar, Mick motioned for Brenda, the bartender for the night. He ordered his favorite beer, then told her to give Darlene whatever she wanted. "Put it on my tab," he said.

When he observed the look Brenda gave him, he lifted his shoulders slightly and offered her an innocent smile. She nodded and leaned across the bar to speak to Darlene. "What can I get you, Hun?"

Darlene tilted her head and replied, "Vodka, water, tall."

Noticing the guys were on the stage setting up, Mick figured it was time for him to join them. He turned to his friend. "You have a nice time tonight, Darlene. Don't let anyone mess with you."

Darlene brushed a strand of hair off her face and offered him a grin. "Don't worry, Mick, I can handle myself. But it is nice that you care."

"Of course, I care. And, yes, I know you can hold your own." Mick realized she knew how to handle herself in a place like this, but still, it got rowdy at times, and he wanted to remind her. Grabbing the beer Brenda had set before him, he took a long drink, then couldn't help but add, "Remember, you can call Henry if you need to."

Darlene glanced toward the big man sitting near the front door. "I'll remember."

"Good." He said as he hugged her. Figuring Darlene was set for the night, he started to walk away.

Darlene grabbed his arm. "Oh, no, you can't leave. Not until you fill me in." She sounded intrigued about something. "Rafe mentioned you've got a new lady. I'm glad. You need someone special in your life."

Her words cut his heart. He tried to cover his feelings with a shrug. "Not anymore. She thinks I'm a jerk."

"Oh. A jerk?" She seemed surprised. "Do you want me to talk to her for you?"

"Darlene, that's probably the worst thing you could do at this point."

"Okay. Still, I offered."

He nodded. "Noted."

"I'm sorry."

"Don't be sorry. Sometimes it just doesn't work." He took another long drink of his beer. "I gotta go," he told Darlene, then set the empty bottle on the counter and headed toward the stage. He didn't need to look back to know she was giving him a sympathetic stare. He could feel her green eyes warming his back.

Ignore it, he thought. After all, everything that happened had been his fault. He'd lied to Reb. He'd wanted her to like him as a fun-loving biker bar musician, not a boring tax attorney. Maybe she'd never know the real him because he didn't know himself right now. He blew out a breath and then pasted on a friendly smile. After all, fans were watching.

Mick stopped at tables along the way to greet the customers who seemed ready to have a good time, drinking, dancing, or listening to music while hanging with friends.

By the time he picked up the microphone, Mick felt good. He glanced around the room and smiled. Mo's had packed in a decent crowd for a weeknight. The music he, and the guys, had prepared earlier excited him. As the countdown started for their first number, adrenaline began to pump through his veins. Yep, they were going to bring down the house.

"Hello, everybody! You ready to have a good time?"

The crowd shouted and cheered at Mick's greeting. Several yelled out their requests.

Mick was in his glory on stage with the mic in his hand. All the stress of his chosen daytime career slipped away as the music filled his soul. Each note and the words he sang released a thrill he had never experienced while preparing financial statements and balancing numbers.

Only one thing could make him happier. To have Reb in the audience smiling at him. Yes, seeing her smile would sure make his night better.

Chapter Nineteen

"Oh, I don't know if this is a good idea." Rebecca shivered and not from being cold. She had expected to be nervous when she walked into Mo's looking for Mick, but her nerves were firing hot needles into her stomach, and her heart was doing aerobics in her chest.

Earlier, she'd agreed with her friends that she should see Mick. Talk things out with him in person. Tell him her side, listen to his. No drama. Talk to each other like adults. Right?

Her decision had seemed correct at the time, but now she wasn't so sure. What if Mick ignored her? Or what if he had a date? Oh, dear, how would she handle that?

Fighting the urge to run and flag down the Uber that had just dropped them off, she took a steadying breath. I need to get my Reb persona back, and I must remember that I'm a strong, confident, kick-ass woman. She straightened her shoulders. Reb can do this. I can do this. Taking a step forward, she yanked open the door.

The four of them walked inside. It was dark, dingy, crowded, and ear-deafening loud.

The big burly guy standing near the entry looked up from his cell phone, "Hey, Rayna. Glad to see you."

Rayna acknowledged his greeting with a cheerful, "Hi, Henry."

He smiled, revealing surprisingly nice teeth. He gave Rebecca and the other two a quick once over. "Ladies, looking good."

Rebecca offered a nod. She thought she heard Scarlett and Trisha both mutter hello. It was too noisy to tell for sure.

Henry, the bouncer, was immense as the broad side of a barn. Both his muscular arms were tattooed from the wrist up to where the ink disappeared under the sleeves of his tight-fitting T-shirt and reappeared along the sides of his massive neck. He'd tied his grey hair back in a low ponytail.

Rebecca felt his eyes following them as they attempted to make their way through the Thursday night crowd. "You know him?" She asked Rayna as soon as they were out of his earshot.

"Of course. Henry's the best. Any trouble, tell him." Rayna added. "He'll handle it."

"Good to know...I guess." Rebecca shivered again. She remembered the fight that had broken out the first time she came to Mo's. However, that was also when she met Mick. Speaking of, she glanced around, trying to find him.

Rayna grabbed Rebecca's hand and pulled her toward the row of tables near the stage area. "Come on," she said loudly. "I see an open table. Let's grab it."

Rebecca glanced over her shoulder to ensure the other two girls followed close behind. They were.

Once seated, Rebecca looked around again. The place was crowded, and she didn't see Mick anywhere. Her stomach tightened. Maybe he had the night off, and all the stress of seeing him was for nothing.

She turned toward the stage. The band's music equipment and instruments were set up. They're on a break. Of course, that explains it. He and the guys probably stepped outside for some air. She remembered Mick had told her that's what they usually did between sets.

Rebecca sucked in a deep breath and let it out. "I need a shot of tequila."

Her friends all broke up laughing.

"What? No butterscotch martini?" Scarlett and Trisha teased in unison.

"Give the girl tequila," Rayna said as she glanced around for a waitress. When she didn't see anyone coming to their table, she pushed back her chair and stood. "I'm going to the bar. I'll get our drinks."

"I'll have a shot," Trisha said.

"Me too," Scarlett added as she held up her hand.

"You got it. Tequila shots all around," Rayna replied. She left the table and headed toward the bar.

It didn't take Rayna long to return with their drinks. She placed four shot glasses onto the table from a serving tray, a bowl of limes, and a saltshaker. "Here you go, ladies. Patrón. Only the best for my girls."

Rebecca picked up the shot glass Rayna had placed in front of her and lifted it to her nose. She took a whiff and grimaced. It smelled strong. Good. Maybe it'll give me courage. She downed it in one gulp.

Rebecca's eyes stung, her throat burned, and her mouth felt like it was on fire. "Damn, that's good," she wheezed.

"Use the lime," Scarlett said as she pushed the bowl of sliced green citrus toward Rebecca.

"Thanks," she croaked. Grabbing a lime wedge, Rebecca shoved it into her mouth and sucked hard. It helped. After a minute, she could breathe normally again.

They all started giggling as, one by one, the other three downed their liquor.

A waitress stopped by the table and took their orders for more tequila. Surprisingly, it didn't take long for her to return with two more shots for each of them. Before long, shot glasses lined up on the table, and laughter erupted as they took turns with the saltshaker and chewed on the limes trying to ease their burning throats.

"We need more tequila—" Rebecca's words abruptly stopped. She let out a sharp gasp. Mick had walked into Mo's by way of the back door.

Rebecca swallowed hard. "He's here," she said. "Mick is here."

They all turned to look in the direction Rebecca was gazing.

"Don't look," she whispered. "Pretend we don't see him."

"How are we supposed to do that? We're sitting right by the stage," Trisha asked.

"I don't know." Rebecca glanced toward the back entrance again.

Yep, Mick had walked in, surrounded by the guys in the band. They were all talking and laughing. A shot of electricity fired through her veins. Mick's dark hair was slightly mussed. Rebecca knew it was because he'd recently run his hands through it. One of his habits. Oh, what she wouldn't give to run her fingers through those dark waves again.

She let out a nervous sigh and straightened in her chair. What will Mick do when he sees me?

The guy who had blocked her whole view of Mick stepped aside as they reached the stage. Rebecca's eyes widened. A tall, smoking, hot redhead held tightly to Mick's arm.

Oh, God, I can't be here. Numbness washed over her, and she couldn't move for a second. Her stomach rolled. "I'm going to be sick."

"What?" Trisha leaned closer to Rebecca. "Are you okay?"

"No." Rebecca scooted down in her seat, trying to shield herself from Mick's view. "I'm going to the restroom."

"Shall we come with you?" Trisha asked.

"Finish your drinks and meet me outside. I want to leave. Now."

"Why? What's going on?" Confusion clearly crossed Trisha's features.

Rayna and Scarlett seemed puzzled as well.

"Where are you going?" Rayna asked.

Rebecca didn't take the time to answer. She slid off her chair, pushed her way through the rows of tables, and tried to blend with the customers standing near the bar. She didn't want to look back, but the minute she heard Mick's voice coming from the stage, it was as if he was a magnet, and she were stainless steel. She couldn't help but turn.

Under the stage lighting, he looked gorgeous. A black T-shirt emphasized his toned muscles, and faded jeans hugged his long legs. Dark hair fell over his forehead as he moved across the stage, holding his audience captive.

I'm such a fool. Rebecca fought the tears forming, and she wasn't about to embarrass herself crying over a band guy in a crummy tavern. She needed to splash some water on her face, call an Uber and go home.

She bolted, turning so fast that she almost collided with a waitress holding a tray of drinks. "Excuse me. I'm sorry," she apologized without stopping until she was inside the safety of the restroom.

Coming here was the worst decision of my life. Rebecca had never felt so miserable. Her heart was broken, her head hurt, and her throat burned from the tequila shots. More tears threatened to spill from her already blood-shot eyes. *She should never have come to Mo's.*

Rebecca glanced around for some tissues. Not finding any, she stepped into a stall, grabbed a fist full of toilet paper, blew her nose, and then splashed water on her face from the faucet of a stained porcelain sink.

The room seemed to spin. Holding onto the edge of the sink for balance, she stared at her reflection in the dirty mirror. Her hair was messy, the waves so carefully arranged earlier were limp and straight, her eyes were puffy, and her lipstick smeared. Not a good look. She grimaced and blinked back another round of tears.

Rebecca wasn't a weepy type. She usually was in total charge of her emotions.

How had she let herself become this pitiful creature at the mercy of a man's attention? She didn't need Mick. She had a great life, good parents, excellent career. Never could she remember a time when she wasn't in complete control of everything until she fell for a band guy. And someone who obviously didn't have deep feelings for her.

No more tears, she told herself. I'm done.

Taking a calming breath, she reached for a paper towel, dried her hands then tossed it into the trash. Standing near the far wall, she fished her phone from the back pocket of her jeans and sent a text requesting an Uber ride. She couldn't wait to get to her parent's house, change into silk pj's, and crawl under the luxurious designer sheets on the big comfy bed.

The restroom door swung open. Three women walked inside. Rebecca offered them a smile, then returned to her phone, hoping the Uber had responded and was on its way.

Suddenly the back of her neck prickled. Feeling eyes on her, she glanced up and noticed one of the women staring at her with a look that made Rebecca uneasy. She forced another smile and started toward the door. But before she had taken more than a few steps, the woman moved to block her way. Rebecca's eyes widened, and her stomach knotted. She'd never been in a fight in her life, but this woman looked like she was ready to start something.

Rebecca quickly assessed her opponent. This is not good. The woman stood at least three inches taller and was probably forty pounds of muscle heavier. Her jet-black hair was pulled tight in a ponytail, and a snake's head tattoo was visible above the V-neck opening of her baggy T-shirt. Rebecca swallowed hard.

Glancing about, she saw the other two women were still there, but both stood near the opposite wall with uninterested expressions. Whose side would they be on if a fight broke out? Rebecca had no idea.

Think. What should she do first? Her phone was still in her hand. She could call for help. But who? Her friends probably wouldn't hear their phones. She could dial 9-1-1. But what would she say? I'm in a biker bar, and a woman is being rude. She had better chances screaming for Henry. Henry. Would he hear if she screamed?

"What are you looking at, Bitch?" The woman's dark eyes flashed, and her words sounded like a snarl.

Rebecca's heart skipped a beat. Hearing the woman's threatening voice roused her ire. She felt like crap, and she'd drank too much. She wanted to go home, and no smart-mouth bully would stop her. Rebecca tilted her head, straightened her shoulders, and voiced her best Reb response. "Do you have a problem with me?"

"Yeah, I don't like your looks, you brunette groupie."

"Excuse me?" That was the wrong thing to say. Rebecca saw a flash of red behind her eyes. "Oh, lady, I am no groupie. If it's a band guy, you want. Be my guest." Rebecca let out a huff and took a step to walk around her.

Again, the woman blocked her. She snarled, "Maybe it's just you I don't like. I saw the way you looked at me."

"I didn't look at you." Rebecca tried again to pass.

"Oh, no." She shoved Rebecca backward. "You're not going anywhere."

Rebecca's face heated. Enough of this crazy person. She clenched her fist. She knew she was no match for this tattooed tank, but she wasn't about to beg for mercy. She'd take a handful of greasy black hair with her if she went down. She gritted her teeth as her muscles tensed, ready to spring forward.

"Back off, Rose." A woman's voice ordered.

Rebecca gasped.

The smoking hot redhead Rebecca had seen with Mick earlier had entered the restroom unnoticed, and now she stood directly beside the woman threatening harm.

Rose? Had the redhead called the tank Rose? The name sure didn't fit the woman.

"Nope." Crazy Rose didn't move. She screwed up her face in a mock grin. "Not happening, Darlene. Not until I settle something with Skinny Barbie."

The hot redhead, now known as Darlene, stepped in front of Rebecca, partly shielding her from the aggressor.

Rose folded her arms across her ample midsection and widened her stance. "Move it, Darlene. This is none of your business."

"I've made it my business," Darlene spoke slowly and steadily. "I took you in high school wrestling, Rosie. I can do it again."

Rose let out a huff.

The two women bystanders who had entered the restroom with Rose moved in closer. One aimed their phone toward them, possibly filming the confrontation. Rebecca still wasn't sure whose side they were on. After all, they had come in at the same time as Rose. Maybe they were her pals? She had no way of knowing for sure. All she knew was she wasn't planning to wait around and find out.

So, what now?

Heart still thudding, she weighed her options. Rebecca took the opportunity to ease a half step sideways with the phone in one hand and the other still clenched. Rose, glaring at Darlene, didn't seem to notice.

It's now or never.

Rebecca bolted for the door.

Yes, I made it.

She ran, crashing into Henry. "Fight in the restroom!"

She didn't wait for Henry's reaction. She kept running until she was in the parking lot, standing next to the wall with the flickering Mo's neon sign.

Rebecca bent at the waist, struggling to catch her breath. Finally, calming down a little, she straightened and saw movement on her left. Someone was approaching, and her heart stilled.

"There you are," Trisha called. "We've been looking for you."

Oh, thank God. Rebecca, still breathing hard, rushed to grab her friend. Hugging her tight, she glanced to see if Rayna and Scarlett were there, and they were. "I've never been so glad to see you guys."

"What's going on?" Rayna asked.

"I was almost killed. That's what." Rebecca took a deep breath, then looked toward the bar's entrance to ensure no one was coming after her.

"Killed?" Rayna's voice sounded strained.

Scarlett let out a breathy gasp.

A dark SUV with tinted windows pulled into the parking lot and eased to a stop.

"Our Uber. Perfect timing." Rebecca released her grip on Trisha's arms and started toward the SUV. "Come on. I'll fill you all in as soon as we're on the road."

Once settled inside the vehicle and it had left the parking lot, Rebecca proceeded to tell her friends about her encounter and the narrow escape from a possible fight.

"How did this start?" Trisha questioned. Her eyebrows knitted together in concern.

"Rose said she didn't like my looks."

"Who's Rose?" Rayna asked.

"The crazy woman who wanted to beat me up. She would have, too, except Darlene came to my rescue."

"Who's Darlene?" Rayna asked as her eyes widened in question.

"The redhead who, I think, was Mick's date." Rebecca snorted.

"Mick had a date?" Scarlett seemed to squeak in surprise.

"That guy is a jerk." Rayna scowled.

"I don't know if he had a date, but I saw her walk in with him, and she was holding onto his arm. Anyway, she helped me get out of the ladies' room."

"Well, we're certainly glad." Trisha patted Rebecca's hand.

"Oh, and get this...crazy Rose called me Skinny Barbie."

A second of silence passed before they all started hysterically laughing, including a chuckle from the Uber driver.

They traveled about a mile before the laughter subsided.

Emotionally drained, Rebecca leaned back against the plush leather seat. "One thing came out of this night. I've decided my old boring life isn't so bad."

"I've never thought your life was bad or boring," Trisha said.

"I'll never go back to that awful place. No offense, Rayna. I know Mo is your cousin." She took a breath and stated firmly, "but I never want to see Mick again."

"You loved him." Trisha spoke quietly, "It's hard to get over a first love."

Rebecca rolled her eyes. "If this is what love feels like, I want no part of it."

"Give yourself some time." Trisha offered a sympathetic smile. "Things will look better in a few days."

Rebecca let out a huff.

The four of them rode the rest of the way in silence. The only sound was a smooth, soulful jazz melody streaming from the Uber driver's radio.

Rebecca turned her head toward the SUV's passenger side window. She stared up through the tinted glass at the crescent moon. Memories of the night she and Mick had made love under a similar moon played in her mind.

I wonder if Mick remembers that night. I guess I'll never know.

Chapter Twenty

Rebecca cracked open her eyes to find Zoey staring at her. The second the dog saw she was awake, she bounced closer and began licking her cheek. "Stop. Enough. I'm awake." She waved her hand in front of her face trying to shield herself from the wet doggie tongue. Zoey was relentless. No matter how often Rebecca attempted to shove the little fur ball away, Zoey jumped right back in her face.

"Oh, Zoey, stop. My head hurts." She tossed back the covers and struggled to sit up. Her head was throbbing, and her mouth felt like someone had stuffed it with cotton. Ugh. I shouldn't have gone to Mo's.

She twisted the edge of her silk pajama top between her fingers as the events from last night surfaced. What if she hadn't been able to escape from Crazy Rose in the restroom? Yikes. She shuddered. And what if she hadn't seen Mick with someone else? Her stomach tightened at the memory. What if...what if.

She felt tears welling up and realized they were because she'd lost Mick. This time for good. "Stop it," she muttered. Crying over him wasn't worth it, and besides, tears wouldn't change anything.

Slowly she stood and glanced at the clock. Oh, no, it can't be this late! "Zoey, I need to get dressed." The little dog cocked her head, jumped off the bed, and headed for the doorway.

Rebecca frowned. Her head was splitting, and she only had twenty minutes to get to the office, or she'd be late for the Friday morning meeting. She needed coffee and strong coffee. Plus, aspirin and the way her head hurt, she'd probably need to take two or three to ease the pain.

She started for the kitchen, hoping her mom still kept the aspirin tablets in the cabinet next to the pantry. Wait? What? Was that coffee she smelled? Her imagination must be working overtime.

She quickened her steps. Entering the kitchen, Rebecca met the fragrant aroma of coffee brewing. Trisha stood next to the stove, and Rayna and Scarlett were there as well. What the heck?

"Good morning," Trisha said brightly. "How are you feeling?"

Startled, Rebecca answered, "Much better now that I see there's a pot of caffeine."

Trisha poured coffee into a mug, then handed it to Rebecca. "It's strong, and Rayna brought us donuts."

"Oh, I love you girls." Rebecca sank into a kitchen chair.

"I hope you like the donuts I picked out." Rayna lifted the lid of a large pink box, revealing an assortment of delicious frosted and glazed treats.

"How did you get in this morning? Did I give you a key?" Rebecca reached for a fluffy glazed donut.

"You insisted we all spent the night," Trisha told her.

"I insisted? I don't remember."

"We didn't want to leave you alone after your experience at Mo's. We kinda feel responsible for talking you into going in the first place."

"I'm certainly glad you stayed, but you didn't force me to go to Mo's. I'm a big girl, and I could have said no." She took a bite and slowly chewed, savoring the sweetness. "So good." She reached for a napkin and then wiped the excess sugar from the tips of two sticky fingers.

"Your mom has flavored creamers in the fridge if you want." Trisha motioned toward the Sub-Zero refrigerator.

"I'm good," Rebecca replied. Her hands shook slightly as she lifted the mug to her lips and sipped. "You're right. Coffee is strong and just what I need."

"Okay, everyone!" Scarlett loudly announced as she stepped into the kitchen from the living room area. "We are all excused from work today."

"What are you talking about? Excused?" Rebecca asked. Scarlett wasn't making sense. She was a little hung over, but still knew today was Friday.

"I called all our workplaces. We're sick." Scarlett wore a pleased expression as she reached for a donut.

"We're all sick?" Rebecca shook her head, still trying to understand what her friend was saying.

"Yep." Scarlett took a bite of a chocolate-frosted donut.

"Well, good," Trisha replied. "I'll make another pot of coffee.

Rebecca heaved a sigh and cocked an eyebrow expressing displeasure, although inwardly, she felt extreme relief.

"You know you're glad you don't have to go to the office today. Admit it," Scarlett teased as she reached for a napkin and wiped drips of chocolate from the table.

It was true Rebecca was glad to miss work today, but she also didn't want to lose her job. Her father had pulled some strings to get her hired as an assistant attorney right after graduation, and she'd hate for him to think she wasn't grateful.

Instead of answering, Rebecca scooted from the chair to find a pain reliever for her headache. Happy to see her mom kept the bottle in the same place as when she still lived at home, she shook two tablets into her hand and then swallowed them with her coffee.

"More coffee anyone?" Rayna asked as she poured herself a second cup, then offered the carafe to the others.

"I'm good." Trisha waved her away.

"Top mine," Scarlett said.

Rebecca shook her head. "No, thanks."

Rayna shrugged, refilled Scarlett's coffee cup, then replaced the carafe onto the coffeemaker.

"I'm going to take a shower." Rebecca rinsed her coffee mug and then placed it in the dishwasher.

Zoey danced around her legs and whined. Rebecca knelt and patted the fluffy-haired little dog's head. "Would one of you mind taking Zoey outside?"

"I will," Rayna said.

"Thank you." Rebecca offered her friend a grateful smile, stood, and headed upstairs.

Rebecca padded straight for the bathroom and turned the shower on full blast. As she removed her pajamas and stepped under the stream of hot water, sighing at how wonderful it felt on her aching muscles, she wondered what Mick was doing right now. She groaned. I'm better off not knowing. She had a feeling the man wasn't sitting around, miserable and lonely. I'll get over him.

She reached for the shampoo bottle, poured a generous amount into her palm, and began massaging her scalp. As the shampoo foamed and bubbled with sweet-smelling suds, Rebecca started belting out, "I'm gonna wash that man right outa my hair," from the movie South Pacific. Ah, if it were only this easy.

Thirty minutes later, Rebecca returned to the kitchen. She'd dressed in a pair of comfy shorts and T-shirt. Her freshly washed hair was pulled up into a messy bun. Thankfully her headache had eased, and she had to admit she felt better except for her darn broken heart, which still hurt.

Rebecca found her friends sitting around the table all working on a jigsaw puzzle. Small pieces of greens, blues, yellow and white were spread out evenly across the tabletop. She leaned over Trisha's shoulder to get a better look. "Humm looks like a romantic Italian landscape."

"It is." Rayna held up the lid to the box showing a picturesque setting from a balcony overlooking the ocean. "Want to join us?"

"I'll just watch." Rebecca moved to an empty spot at the table.

"Feeling better?" Trisha asked as she matched a puzzle piece to another in the same shade of blue. It fit perfectly.

"I guess I do. For a person whose life is over," Rebecca answered as she eased into the chair.

Trisha laughed, then replied without looking up, "You're always saying that." She seemed to be on a roll finding the right pieces, and her corner of the puzzle was filling in nicely.

"This time, I mean it." Rebecca rested her elbows on the table and leaned forward, cupping her chin with her hands.

Trisha glanced up and studied her for a moment. "Well, your life's not over; however, I think you need to make some changes."

"Changes?" Rebecca picked up a white puzzle piece. "Like what?" She asked while toying with it.

Trisha asked quietly, "Rebecca, what would make you happy? And I'm not talking about Mick, I'm referring to your career choice."

"I'm happy." Rebecca frowned. She tossed the puzzle piece she'd been holding back into the pile. She stared at Trisha, realizing her friend was serious. "Where's this question coming from?"

Trisha met her gaze. "Only an observation. You're constantly complaining."

"I don't mean to gripe." She shrugged and nodded. "You know, Trisha, I've thought about private practice.

"It's almost lunchtime," Rayna interrupted. "I'll go pick us up something."

"Great idea," Scarlett added. "I'll go with you."

"Any preferences? Salads, sandwiches?" Rayna glanced at Rebecca and then at Trisha.

"Surprise us," Trisha stated.

"Rebecca added, "Anything works for me. Take my car. The keys are on the counter."

Scarlett and Rayna grabbed their purses and keys, then headed toward the door.

Once they were alone, Trisha turned to Rebecca again and softly asked, "Private practice is a great idea. Maybe your parents can help, and I'll bet your dad will be for it."

"I've been giving it some serious thought. Please don't mention it to the others yet. I'm still on the fence."

"You have time."

"I just feel so confused."

"I think that's one of the reasons you're so attracted to Mick. He's different, and you're looking for someone to make you happy."

"Doesn't everyone want someone to make them happy?"

"Yes. But true happiness comes from inside yourself. You won't find it being someone you're not. We've had fun dressing up and going out, but that's pretending. If you want true happiness, look inside your heart. Be your authentic self. Remember in college how you talked about having your own office? Follow your dreams, Rebecca."

Rubbing her forehead, Rebecca admitted honestly, "Oh, Trisha, the problem is I don't know what I want anymore."

"Well, you don't seem to have any passion for your position with Whitaker Law. Am I right?" Trisha shrugged. "I think you're still trying to make your parents happy."

Rebecca felt her face heat. She blew out a breath and brought forth her best professional smile. The one that said everything's okay, I'm in control, and how may I help you, smile. "Making my parents proud is how I've always lived my life, and it's hard to change."

Why was it so hard to voice what was in her heart? Trisha was warm, honest, and a wonderful friend who would listen and never make judgments. It was true. Her father had planned her life for her since she was a little girl. His dream was for her to follow in his footsteps. Enter the political world as he had when he was her age. He'd already opened the doors by arranging the prestigious job with Whitaker Law. In truth, she'd prefer a law practice of her own where she could help women in need of a new and better life. It was the women staying at The Haven that she'd like to represent.

"Of course, you want to honor your parent's wishes, but you must also make yourself happy. Just promise you'll think about what you truly desire. And as for Mick, leave him out of the equation. Your relationship with him will work out on its own for the best. Some things are simply meant to be...or not."

Rebecca gave a half-hearted sigh. "I will do some soul searching. I promise."

"Remember, if you need a friend to run an idea by, I'm a good listener."

Rebecca reached over and hugged her. "Thank you."

The front door opened.

"Yoo hoo. Lunch is here," Scarlett announced.

Scarlett and Rayna walked in, holding restaurant carry-out bags that looked filled to the brim with Styrofoam cartons.

It didn't take long for the four to be seated around the dining table. Large grilled chicken and vegetable salads, several containers of humus in assorted flavors, and plates of crispy pita chips covered the tabletop. Everything looked delicious.

"Hey, I know what will make lunch better. Wine." Rebecca headed for the cabinet where her parents kept the liquor. She selected three bottles from the shelf and headed back to the table. Placing the selection of wine in the center between the food, she turned and hurried to grab some wine glasses.

Before long, each friend lifted their glass, clinked gently, and made a toast.

Rebecca closed her eyes for a second before taking a sip. Please give me the strength to not show how much I'm hurting over Mick.

"Look!" Rayna screamed, "Rebecca, you're famous." She'd been playing on her phone while the girls filled their plates. Now she hopped up and down in her chair. "You've gone viral. Here, check this out."

Staring in disbelief at the video on Rayna's phone, Rebecca almost choked on her wine. After coughing and catching her breath, she stammered, "What the hell?"

"Wow. Viral." Trisha said as her eyes widened. "Who posted it?"

"It's on Mo's social media site." Rayan had settled down and passed her phone from one girl to the next. "Man, that woman is a tank. Rebecca, you're lucky she didn't kill you."

"I told you she was scary. Let me see it again." Rebecca pried the phone from Scarlett's fingers and hit replay. Immediately the video opened with Rose harassing Rebecca in the restroom at Mo's.

Oh, my gosh. Oh, holy crap.

"Rayna, do something. Get Mo to take this down." Rebecca's mind whirled. What would happen if her boss saw this online? Or her parents! Oh, no, my dad will have a fit.

"Rebecca, what's Mo supposed to do? I mean, he didn't take the video." Rayna stated. Her words sounded like an apology.

211

"Mo's your cousin, and he should have a say in the matter." Rebecca pleaded, "You have to ask him."

"Okay, but I don't know..." Rayna shrugged, "I'll try. I guess he can take it off his social media page. That might help you."

"Thank you. Anything will help. Oh, this is awful." Rebecca pushed back her chair and stood. "I need another aspirin."

"I'll go and see Mo right now," Rayna promised as she glanced at her watch. "Maybe I can catch him before the Friday night crowd comes in."

"Actually, Rebecca, you look good in the video." Scarlett's words held a hint of pride. "See this. Here's where Rebecca is called Skinny Barbie." Scarlett held the phone up and hit replay again. "You stood up to that bully. I bet you'd have belted Rose a good one if Darlene hadn't come in when she did."

Trisha raised her eyebrows in agreement. "It does look that way. Everyone, meet Rebecca Badass."

Her friends laughed together, watching the video for the fifth time as they passed the remaining bottle of wine around, refilling their glasses.

Rebecca groaned. "Badass." Exactly what I need on my resume.

###

Mo's was different during the day. It was still dark and dingy, but it was quiet at three o'clock in the afternoon and smelled of stale beer and greasy food. As Mick's eyes adjusted to the darkness, he noticed the place was almost empty of customers. Brenda, the bartender, had her back turned to him while taking inventory of the liquor bottles lining the wall behind the bar. A couple of regulars were at a corner table drinking beer and eating finger food from a red plastic basket. Three old guys were over by the pool table.

Mo sat at the bar with his laptop open. On the stool next to him was a curvy young lady, her hair shimmered pink under the bar's low lights.

Mo waved him over. "Look at this. Mo's is going crazy on the social media scene."

Mick sauntered up to the bar. "I stay off social media."

His brow furrowed. Mick didn't have time for casual chit-chat this afternoon. He'd only stopped in to pick up some paperwork from Mo. The owner needed help with his tax forms. He still had to return to his office for an appointment with a new client who could only see him late in the day. If lucky, it wouldn't last long, and he'd have time to grab a bite to eat and relax a few minutes before he had to be back at Mo's tonight. This part-time job of filling in for band members was turning out to be full-time.

Mick figured it was time for a serious talk with Rafe. He thought he'd made it clear. He was only to fill in when a regular band guy couldn't make it. As it was now, he was singing or sitting in for someone four nights a week. He was starting to wonder how seriously Rafe was looking for another permanent band member. Nights at Mo's, then getting to the office the following day was becoming harder and harder. Something had to give.

"Pull up a stool. Have a beer. Brenda, get Mick a beer," Mo ordered.

"No, really," Mick protested, but Brenda sat a frosted mug of draft on the bar in front of him anyway. Resigned to the moment, he grabbed the mug and took a long swig. The cold beer tasted good.

"Mick, you know my cousin Rayna." Mo turned toward the lady sitting next to him.

The pink-haired lady offered Mick a smile.

Nodding politely, Mick answered, "Nice to see you." He wasn't sure he knew her, but she did look familiar. He just couldn't put his finger on when he'd seen her before. It would come to him, he had a good memory for faces.

"You should watch the video," Rayna told him. "You might find it interesting."

"Yeah, Mick. Take a look." Mo laughed. "Rose was up to her old tricks last night, and she drank too much and tried to start something."

Mick placed his beer on the bar. "Mo, why do you keep serving that woman? One of these days, she's going to cause a real problem."

"I know. I know." Mo shrugged. "Henry gave her a talk. She's eighty-sixed until she can control herself."

"She gets mean when she drinks." Mick picked up his beer and downed the last of it. "Do you have your paperwork ready for me? I've got an appointment."

"Yeah, yeah. Brenda." Mo leaned closer to the bar. "Get the manila folder on my desk. Pretty please."

Pretending to be annoyed, Brenda headed toward the back office.

Mo chuckled as Brenda left. "She's one hot mama. Check out that ass." He gave a low whistle.

Mick grinned. He'd known those two had something going on between them for a long time. It was apparent to anyone who spent time around them.

Brenda returned shortly and handed the folder to Mo.

Mick smiled, noticing their fingers touched briefly.

"Mick," Rayna scooted off the stool and stepped to his side. "Will you check out the video? I'm trying to get Mo to take it down, and I'd like your opinion."

"I'd like to hear what you think, too," Mo added.

Mick frowned. They weren't going to give up until he watched a lousy video of Rose drunk. "Sure. Let's have a look."

Mo turned the laptop toward Mick and pushed play.

The video started with Rose making nasty comments to a smaller person. Typical, Mick thought. Nothing worse than a woman who can't hold her liquor, trying to intimidate some innocent victim. He shook his head.

The camera turned and zoomed in on the girl Rose was harassing. Mick's breath caught. His pulse skyrocketed as he watched the brunette beauty staring wide-eyed toward the woman threatening her harm. Reb? What the hell? Reb is the one threatened by Rose.

Mick's mind whirled as questions peppered into his mind. Why was Rose bothering Reb? How did he not see that she was here? Trying to focus on the video, he leaned closer to the screen. Reb trembled as she straightened her back, trying to stand her ground. Damnit. Good thing Rose isn't here right now. His hand slapped the bar top.

Mick shot his attention to Rayna.

"Yes, Mick, that's Rebecca. My friend is getting harassed by Rose."

Mick's eyes widened as recognition hit. That night he met Reb, she'd been with her girlfriends, including this girl with pink hair. Rayna. His mind clicked. She was also the friend who'd been in an accident, and Reb left to go to the hospital.

"Yep." She'd moved closer and met his stare. "It's me. I was here the night you met Rebecca, and I was also here with her last night."

"Is Reb okay? Why didn't I know she came in?"

Mick couldn't pry his eyes from the video. Darlene came in and stepped between Rose and Reb. They exchanged words, then Reb disappeared from the screen. Henry barreled in and grabbed Rose. The camera flipped to the ceiling and then to the floor showing booted feet and the dirty tiles until Henry shouted to turn the phone off.

"Maybe you would have known if she hadn't seen you with another woman." Rayna let out an indignant huff.

"I...I wasn't with anyone," Mick stammered. "How did Reb get that crazy idea?" What did I do to make her think I was with someone? He played the events of the night in his mind.

"Oh, I don't know. Maybe because Rebecca saw you arm-and-arm with someone when you came in from your break."

Oh, no, Darlene. "Reb thought I was with Darlene?"

Laughter erupted from Mo. He turned to Rayna. "Darlene would more than likely be hitting on you than Mick."

"Darlene's only a friend. Not a date." Mick shook his head.

"Oh." Rayna was speechless for a second. Her eyes widened as she glanced from Mick to Mo, then back to Mick. "Well, this is awful. Rebecca thought, well, she figured, oh, wow."

Mick grabbed his phone and hit the number programmed for Reb. His heart hammered as he waited for it to connect. "What! She's got me call blocked."

"Oh, sorry, Mick. Yeah, she said she was going to do that." Rayna lifted her shoulders.

"Okay, well, that's it. I'm going to Reb's house. I've got to straighten this out."

"Mick, Rebecca isn't at home. She's staying at her parent's while they're on a cruise."

"What's the address?"

"I can't give it to you. She'd kill me." Rayna let out a breath. "Sorry."

"Then, can you convince her to talk to me?" Mick was desperate and couldn't let it end between them like this. He had lots to explain, and he still owed her an apology for the previous misunderstanding.

"I'll do my best. She's pretty hurt. I'm not sure she'll consider coming here, not after last night."

Mick nodded. "Yeah, I get it."

"Is there anything I can do?" Mo offered.

"I wish I knew of something. Thanks anyway."

Mick couldn't hide his hopelessness. At this point, what choice did he have? All Mick could do was wait and hope Rayna could explain the facts to Reb and bring her to Mo's. If not, his other option was to wait until Monday and show up at her office. He would do whatever it took to make things right between them, he had to.

Mick picked up the folder of Mo's tax paperwork and gestured with it as he spoke. "See you later." He'd like to hang around and plead his case to Rebecca's friend, but he had to leave for his client appointment.

Mo nodded.

Rayna smiled.

As Mick strode across the parking lot toward his car, he couldn't help but ponder how fast his day had gone from bad to worse. All because he'd pretended to be the man, he'd thought Reb wanted.

Chapter Twenty-One

Rebecca thought she was doing a fair job of hiding her heartbreak over Mick from her friends. She joked, played games, and helped add pieces to the giant puzzle along with Trisha and Scarlett. Of course, the wine she drank helped her forget about the scary Rose event, but the Mick problem, nothing seemed to ease the pain. Her heart was shattered.

Finding out he'd been less than honest about his life had angered her, but it hadn't broken her heart the way seeing him with someone else had. Darlene holding on to his arm had been the icing on the cake. The sight of Mick moving on with another woman meant she'd genuinely lost him. Maybe worse yet, she'd never actually had him.

Their relationship had only been fun and games for him. He was good, though, she admitted, she'd fallen for him hook, line, and sinker, believing every deceitful word. Pathetic. Rebecca sighed, reached across the table, and poured herself another wine.

Rebecca glanced at the clock. Where the heck was Rayna? She should be back by now with news that Mo deleted the video. He might not have a say about removing it everywhere on the internet, but at least it wouldn't be so available. Oh, who was she kidding? Everyone could still see it. She took a long swallow of wine.

I'll try to stay optimistic. After all, even if someone she knew happened to see it, they probably wouldn't recognize her. Who did she know who'd expect to see her at Mo's? Her friends all went to the Ritz.

I wish my parents were back, Rebecca sighed. Her mom would have all the answers. "This is silly. I don't need to run to mom," she whispered aloud. After all, she was a strong, independent adult woman. She was an attorney, for bloody sakes, representing clients with real honest-to-goodness problems. She didn't give a flip about a stupid video of an inebriated bully harassing her. And most of all, she didn't care about the fake bad boy musician Mick Harris. She finished the glass of wine and reached for the bottle. It was empty.

"Are you okay?" Scarlett asked.

Rebecca stood, looked at her friend, and brushed a strand of hair off her face that had escaped her updo. "Never better. Except I'm out of wine."

Sighing, Rebecca went to check out her mom's wine cabinet, and found a bottle of Pinot Noir that looked appealing. She turned back toward the dining room as the back door opened, and Rayna walked in.

"Thank goodness. I was getting worried." Rebecca arched an eyebrow. "So, what did you find out? Will Mo take down the video?"

"It's a long story. Pour me a glass of that wine, and I'll fill you in." Rayna tossed her handbag on the kitchen counter and headed toward the dining room where the others were waiting.

Once seated, Rebecca filled Rayna's glass and asked, "So what did Mo say?"

"Mo said he'll delete the video from his social media." She took the glass Rebecca offered.

"Good." Rebecca breathed a sigh of relief. "Thank you for going and asking him."

"You're welcome." Rayna took a sip of the wine, then said, "Here's the good part. I saw Mick."

"What!" Rebecca's eyes widened. "You talked to him?"

"I did. Guess what? Darlene wasn't a date."

Rebecca blinked.

Rayna nodded. "It's true. I believe him."

Rebecca's stomach clenched. "I don't understand. You asked him if Darlene was his date?"

"Well, you had to be there to know how it happened. See, Mick was watching the video—"

"He watched the video!" Rebecca blurted, cutting off Rayna's words. "How the heck? Who showed it to him? And why was he at Mo's during the day?" Rebecca couldn't believe what she was hearing.

"Let Rayna explain," Trisha said.

"Yes. I want to hear this," Scarlett agreed.

Rebecca filled her glass and passed the bottle to her friends. She took a drink, closed her eyes, and said, "Go ahead. Let's hear what happened."

The three women listened intently as Rayna filled them in on how Mo had insisted Mick watch the video. Then how shocked he'd been when he realized it was Rebecca that Rose was harassing.

Rayna took a breath, then described how the subject of Darlene had come about. Finally, Rayna offered a smile. "I'm convinced Mick and Darlene are only friends."

A single tear trickled down Rebecca's cheek as she listened intently to Rayna, describing how upset Mick had been when she refused to give him her parent's address.

"Mick cares about you," Rayna added, "he said he was afraid if you knew he was a tax attorney, you'd dismiss him as just another boring guy. He wanted to show you he could be exciting." She shook her head. "He was genuinely upset, and I saw firsthand how crushed he was finding out you'd call blocked him."

Rebecca cringed. "I forgot I did that."

"Maybe you should call him," Trisha said softly.

"You should," Scarlett agreed. "It sounds like he wants to talk."

"Seriously, he does. You should listen to what he has to say." Rayna leaned closer and rested her hand on Rebecca's arm. "Think about it."

Rebecca's head was spinning from everything Rayna had told her. Was it possible Mick cared about her, and this entire mess between them had been caused by miscommunications, misunderstandings, and maybe a little bit of left-out details?

She rolled the wine glass stem between her fingers, deep in thought, and a wave of regret passed through her. The problem started with her wanting a new and more exciting life, and Mick had given it to her. Maybe she was being unfair. One thing was for sure. She couldn't leave things as they were. So, what would it hurt to grant him the chance to explain his side? After all, didn't he deserve that much?

Rebecca rubbed her temples. She had to think of something other than a simple phone call. She needed to come up with an original idea. Something different that Mick wouldn't be expecting. Her father always told her, 'if you want something bad enough, you'll find a way.' And really, what did she have to lose? At this point, she may as well give it her best shot. If there were nothing between them, at least she'd know for sure and not live her life wondering, what if. She took a deep breath and closed her eyes. You'll find a way, she repeated inside her mind.

Seconds ticked by.

Rebecca opened her eyes and turned toward her friends. A smile quirked the corners of her mouth. Meeting their questioning stares, she cocked her head. "Nope, I'm not going to call him." She lifted her wine glass. "I have a wild idea."

Rebecca's nerves were buzzing under her skin by late afternoon on Saturday. She'd devised the perfect plan to take Mick's breath away. She'd walk into Mo's tonight dressed in the outfit she'd worn the first time she'd gone to the biker bar. The night she'd met Mick. Inhaling and then releasing a deep breath, she smiled. "This is going to be fantastic."

Laughter filled her bedroom as the girls sipped wine and applied the finishing touches to their makeup. She'd also talked her friends into wearing the same outfits they'd worn that night. Everything had to be perfect.

Rebecca showed the girls the leather top she'd found tucked away in her closet. Then she brought out the blonde wig.

"You're wearing the wig too?" Trisha asked.

"Yep. I haven't worn it since." Rebecca held it up. "I want to surprise Mick. Will it do the trick?"

"Absolutely. We're recreating the night at Mo's." Scarlett twirled a piece of her hair around the curling iron. "Fingers crossed there's no bar fight."

"I'm not taking any bets on that not happening. After all, it is Mo's." Rebecca's mind began spinning with memories of Rose threatening her in the restroom. Then back to the first night when all hell broke loose, and Mick had to rescue her from being in the middle of the brawl. She shivered. "All I know is I've been there twice, and both times there's been an altercation of some sort."

"Great," Trisha replied sarcastically. "Are we sure we want to do this?"

"Yes," Rebecca answered. "It's a great plan. I want to show Mick I'm wild and adventuresome. Plus, a little unpredictable." She unfastened her bra, tossed it onto the bed, then pulled the leather shirt over her head. She turned to the full-length mirror. "Yikes, I forgot how low-cut this top is. Am I showing too much?"

"We had this conversation the last time you wore it," Scarlett reminded her. "It's not too racy. It's just right."

"Perfect," echoed Trisha.

"It definitely makes me feel sexy," Rebecca murmured.

"Do we have any more glitter anywhere? I think I wore a lot that night." Scarlett reached for the wine glass she'd placed on the dresser earlier.

"Yes, Scarlett, you were undeniably sparkling," Rayna said as she wiggled into her black jeans.

Rebecca hurried into the bathroom, opened a vanity drawer, and grabbed a small plastic container. Then walking back to Scarlett, she tossed a handful of glitter at her. Sparkles of silver, pink, and purple rained over Scarlett's freshly crimped hair and across her bare shoulders. Rebecca howled in laughter at her friend's surprised expression.

Two hours later, each of them had recreated their personas from the first night they'd set foot in Mo's.

Rebecca fastened the clasp on her bracelet, then glanced into the full-length mirror and smiled at her reflection. "Oh my gosh, everyone. Look at us."

The others crowded in front of the mirror and nodded their approval.

"Wow," Rebecca murmured. "Perfect."

Rayna wore her skinny jeans and tight T-shirt with the skull and angel wings on the back. She'd added several additional pink hair extensions to her already pink-dyed curls, and the look was stunning.

Scarlett wore a low-cut top and skirt with a hem that fluttered around her calves. She'd even remembered to wear her silver, dangling fairy earrings. And with all the multi-colored glitter in her hair and body, she truly sparkled.

Trisha's dark hair flowed around her shoulders in loose shiny waves. Her lips were full and pouty with her favorite cherry lip gloss. Her outfit was a short red dress, showing off her toned bare legs. She looked beautiful.

Rebecca cast her gaze to herself. "Oh," she whispered. It was as if she'd stepped back in time. Wearing an extremely low-cut leather halter top with the sheer lace insert, a pair of skin-tight jeans, four-inch sandals, and her long platinum wig, she almost didn't recognize herself.

She blinked. If this outfit doesn't get Mick's attention, nothing will.

Chapter Twenty-Two

It was taking nearly forty-five minutes for their Uber to drive the usual twenty minutes from her parent's home to Mo's bar. Rebecca had never seen such backed-up traffic delays, even on her daily commute to downtown Phoenix.

It was because of the work being done on the Westbound 101 freeway, and it had been diverted down to one lane. Then due to someone having a fender bender, the one designated lane had to be rerouted to a side street until traffic could get back on the freeway. Their Uber driver explained in detail why it was taking them so long to reach their destination.

Rebecca glanced at her watch for the fifth time in the last ten minutes. She didn't care about the reasons. She wanted results. Couldn't he have found a better route? *If I was driving, we'd already be at Mo's enjoying our first drink. And be with Mick, maybe.*

Finally, they reached their destination. Rebecca began to tremble as they stepped from the car and walked toward the entrance to Mo's. Her nerves were raging. What if this night didn't go as she had planned? She hadn't made a backup plan, in case. What was wrong with her? She always made a plan B.

"I'm worried. What if this doesn't work?" Rebecca asked her friends as they stood near the entrance to Mo's.

"You won't know if we don't go inside," Rayna replied. "Come on."

"Wait!" Rebecca grabbed her arm.

Rayna took Rebecca by the hand. "This is your idea." She pulled her through the opened door, followed closely by the others.

Yes, I absolutely can. Rebecca squared her shoulders, lifted her chin, and strutted what she knew was her hot little body through Mo's crowd of mostly inebriated people.

"I've reserved the table we sat at that night," Rayna announced. "We're going to do everything the same."

"Almost everything," Rebecca quirked a brow. "I have a few differences planned."

They all laughed as they seated themselves around the corner table.

As soon as Rebecca slid into her chair, she immediately checked her surroundings. The band was rocking out with a current Luke Combs chart-topping tune, and Mick was singing to a crowd of lovelies clapping their hands in time to the beat. Several couples were making their way around the dance floor, and the rest of the customers were just plain rowdy.

Rebecca let out a pent-up breath.

It's now or never.

She scooted from the table and stepped onto the dance floor after getting a thumbs-up from her friends. Immediately she was surrounded by dancers, and she zigzagged her way through them to stop near the corner edge of the stage.

Mick had his eyes directed to the other side of the room. Rebecca's heartbeat quickened as she watched him. Overwhelming emotion bubbled up inside her. What was it about this man? It was as if he held her suspended in time, in space, just like the first time she saw him. She couldn't help but wonder, would she always feel like this? Have this raw physical yearning for every part of him, right here and now.

As the song ended, the crowd burst into loud clapping and cheering. Mick moved to the center of the stage. "Thanks, everybody." He smiled, then added, "We've got time for one more before we take a short break. Do I hear any requests?"

"I have one."

Mick's head whipped toward the female voice. His heart skipped as his eyes lasered on the vision before him. Dressed in tight jeans that hugged her slender hips, a low-cut top that pushed her perky breasts toward him, long blonde hair flowing over her shoulders in shiny waves, and full red lips. She looked like a supermodel. Oh yeah, even wearing her blonde wig, he'd know her anywhere. And she was smiling, the dazzling one that took his breath away.

She stepped forward and held out her hand. "Hi, I'm Rebecca Prentice. An assistant attorney at Whittaker Law firm."

Mick took her slender, delicate hand in his. "Nice to meet you, Rebecca." His voice sounded throaty to his ears.

"You may call me Reb."

"Reb. Yeah, I like that." He couldn't believe she'd made herself look exactly like the first time they'd met. Only this time, he wasn't going to make a mistake. Common sense told him to go slow and easy, but as he stared into her smoky eyes, his body seemed to have a mind of its own.

Leaning close, he whispered, "Mick, also known as Michael Harris, tax attorney. I'm glad you came tonight. I wasn't sure you would." His eyes roamed over the length of her. "I love your outfit, and it's the same one you wore the night we met."

"I'm glad you like it." Her tone was soft like velvet. "I've missed you." She gave a little shrug. "I'm sorry about everything."

Memories of their time together played across his mind. How much they'd laughed at each other's silliness. And the feel of her smooth skin, the taste of her mouth, the sweet smell of her body after making love. A strong desire that he couldn't contain rushed through him. "I love you," he admitted. His breath caught, was he being honest about his feelings too soon? Sweat formed along his forehead as he mentally prepared for rejection.

Reb's pouty lips slowly curved into a smile, then meeting his gaze, answered softly, "I love you, too."

Mick blinked as joy filled his heart. He grabbed her and hugged her tightly while kissing her with all the emotion he possessed.

Around them, the bar full of bikers, music lovers, and folks simply out having a good time hooted and cheered. Someone in the back of the bar whistled loudly.

Rebecca was the one to break their kiss. Then with a devilish tilt of her head, she batted her eyelashes and boldly asked, "So, are you going to sing to me or what?"

Mick couldn't help but laugh. Turning to the guys, he gave them a sign for the song he wanted them to play. As soon as the downbeat started, he spoke into his microphone, "This one is for my girlfriend."

Music began to swirl around them. And Mick sang the words straight from his heart.

"Tonight. Who knew...I'd find you here tonight?"

He pulled Reb in closer, and they began to move together in perfect sync to the beat.

"Waiting for so long, for someone...for you. Because you're beautiful...tonight."

Epilogue

Maui was beautiful this time of year. Rebecca let out a dreamy sigh as she gazed up into the brilliant summer sky. Clouds were beginning to build, and the afternoon trade winds were picking up, blowing a warm breeze across her tanned skin.

Rebecca was stretched out on a lounge chair, wearing a yellow string bikini, on the private terrace of Mick's luxurious Hawaiian condo. She turned her head and gazed toward the stunning view of the ocean waves as they lapped against a white sand beach.

The patio glass door slid open. "Hey, would my fiancée like a Butterscotch Martini?"

"Yum." Shading her eyes with her hand, she looked up to see Mick standing next to the lounger holding a fancy cocktail in each hand. "Wow. You made these?"

"I did. If I do say so myself, I'm getting quite good as a bartender."

Rebecca pulled herself up into a sitting position and took one from his outstretched hand. "Well, I'll be the judge." She let her eyes close as she took a sip, then smacked her lips. A smile stretched the corners of her mouth as she opened her eyes and whispered, "Perfect."

"I need to know how to make a drink my lady likes. And since I'm partners with Mo now, I might be called in to play bartender occasionally." He lowered himself onto the lounge chair and ran his fingers over her thigh.

She let out a soft gasp when his fingers, still chilled from holding the cocktail, touched her skin. "No bartending." She parted her legs slightly. "You're only to sing and keep his books balanced." She laughed. "Lord knows Mo needs help in that area." She took another sip of her martini, then placed it on the table next to the lounger. With a tilt of her head, she added, "Besides, you're going to be very busy helping plan our wedding."

Mick set his drink aside then, leaning close, whispered, "You think your girlfriends will let me have a say about anything?" He ran the back of his fingers gently across her thigh.

A little sigh of pleasure escaped before she managed to answer, "Of course. At least one or two things. I'll insist."

"You plan whatever makes you happy. Just let me know where to be and when to show up."

"Oh, no. You're not getting off that easy. You're planning this wedding with me every step of the way. And I have something different and exciting in mind. Maybe even wild."

"Wild? Should I be scared?"

"Maybe, just a little." She gave him a mischievous grin.

Mick winced and then muttered, "Wait a minute, we're not getting married by an Elvis impersonator, are we?"

"Why not? You're my hunka, hunka, burnin' love."

The look of shock on his face caused her to laugh. Rebecca arched her eyebrows. "Viva Las Vegas, baby."

"Well," Mick cleared his throat and, offering his best Elvis impression, said, "Woman, you set my soul on fire."

"Okay, okay. No Elvis, but our wedding will be spectacular."

Mick exhaled a sigh. He pressed a hand over his heart. "You know, I love you tender, baby."

"Stop!" She slapped his shoulder playfully.

"Ah, Reb, don't be cruel." A smile kicked up the corners of his mouth. "Hey, I'm on a roll."

"Uh, no," She shook her head and replied casually. "Keep it up, and I will find us an Elvis preacher."

Mick shuddered. "Elvis has left the building."

He leaned forward and pressed his lips to hers. After several seconds, he pulled away and gazed into her eyes. His expression turned serious. "Honey, you might want to think about hiring a wedding planner. Starting your private law practice, you'll have your hands full, and I'm not sure you'll have time to plan a wedding, a honeymoon, and a grand opening."

"No worries. As far as my law practice goes, my parents have everything under control. Dad is meeting with the contractor tomorrow to finalize the new flooring, and mom is working with an interior decorator. They'll have my office ready for business whenever I am." She reached for her drink. "Plus, I'm already taking resumes for a paralegal." She sent him a saucy look and then ran a finger along the rim of the glass before taking a sip. "This really is delicious."

Mick smiled. "I'm glad you approve of my bartending talents, and I'm also happy that you're close to your parents. Family is important."

"I'm their only child, and they live to run my life." Rebecca laughed. "I've figured out how to deal with them, though." She tilted her head slightly and raised her eyebrows. "I just let them think they're the ones making my decisions. Besides, having them help around the office will keep them both out of trouble."

"Hmm," he mumbled as he noticed her eyes twinkling. "Looks like I'm going to have my hands full with you." Mick began trailing kisses down her throat.

"Mmm," she moaned. "I'm going to love being married to you." Rebecca ran her fingers along his cheek.

Mick gazed down at her as he turned his head and pressed a kiss into her palm. "I'm going to be the best husband you can imagine."

Pleasure rippled through her at his promise. She gave him a wicked smile. "I have a creative imagination."

"Yeah. I know you do." He leaned in and gave her a long mind-blowing kiss. When the kiss ended, he lifted his head and gazed into her eyes. "Start working on a list of creative things you want this husband of yours to do."

She wiggled her eyebrows suggestively. "I'm still working on my list of the things I want from my groom-to-be."

Mick laughed, stood, and reached for her hand. "Let's go inside. You can start showing me some of the things on your list." He pulled her up into his arms. "Later, we'll take a ride along the beach, and you can let your hair blow in the ocean breeze."

"I'm beginning to enjoy riding on your Harley. I love that you keep one here in Maui for vacations."

"All the luxury of working hard."

She nodded in agreement.

Holding her to his chest, he whispered, "I'm crazy in love with you, my beautiful, wild-hearted Reb."

As Rebecca leaned against him, breathing in his masculine scent, she closed her eyes and smiled. She finally knew exactly who she was, and right now, she figured she was the luckiest woman in the world.

The End

Readers we need you.

Please leave a review, even a one liner counts, and has a big influence on our future sales.

Dani Petrone has loved writing for as long as she can remember. A shy girl, she escaped into worlds where she expressed herself by writing, mostly about kittens and horses. As a teenager, her interests turned to boys, and the stories became a romance. As a published author, she considers herself blessed to work from home barefoot and wearing pj's.

Dani lives in Arizona, near her children and grandkids. When not writing, she's drinking butterscotch martinis with her author friends, wasting time on social media, or binge-watching suspense movies. She enjoys touring luxury homes, exploring haunted hot spots, and taking scenic road trips. She's an active member of several writing groups, including a founding member of The Butterscotch Martini Girls.

Dani divides her writing time between her own books and those she writes as half of the writing team, Tia Dani

Tia Dani from BWL Publishing, Inc.

Death Unseen
The Prophecy – Vada Gambit, Book 1
The Deception – Vada Gambit, Book 2
Time's Enduring Love
Call Down the Darkness

BWL Publishing

bwlpublishing.ca